"Please." Anna put her hand on his arm. "Tell me, my lord, please, do not torture me this way. Tell me, before we go in—what will you do?"

Crewe placed his hand over hers and turned to look into her pale face, into eyes huge and deep with fear, at lips tremulous and beseeching. He almost kissed her. Instead he smiled.

"So long as I find you beautiful, I shan't tell your little secret. It shall be between us."

"What does that mean?"

"It means, my dear . . . that I shall have the undoubted pleasure of having you in my power."

"That . . . you cannot do that . . . that would be cruel," she said, gasping.

He looked down into her face and smiled. "But not without its pleasures . . ."

Thief of Love

Linda Walker

JOVE BOOKS, NEW YORK

THIEF OF LOVE

A Jove Book / published by arrangement with
the author

PRINTING HISTORY
Jove edition / June 1994

ISBN: 0-515-11355-7

A JOVE BOOK®
Jove Books are published by The Berkley Publishing Group,
200 Madison Avenue, New York, New York 10016.
JOVE and the "J" design are trademarks
belonging to Jove Publications, Inc.

PRINTED IN THE UNITED STATES OF AMERICA

10 9 8 7 6 5 4 3 2 1

For Max and Sam
with joy and love.

Chapter One

OUTSIDE THE SMALL cottage the howling wind tore at the trees and flung rain against the windowpanes. Anna Farrant shivered and drew her shawl tighter. The thin curtains billowed in the draft. She raised her hand to cup the candle flame as it sputtered and threatened to go out. The fire was low; she considered trying to rouse it to flame but was tired and unwilling to waste more coal on the night's futile enterprise.

She scowled at the figures she had added and subtracted and added and subtracted again, but no matter how many ways she arranged them, the outcome never changed: There was almost no money left.

The last of the proceeds from the sale of her garnet eardrops was gone, chasing the money from her precious pianoforte. There were still the books—but so few now!—and her wages from the Hall. They had in hand three pounds, no more than that. She would have to sell the pearls.

And when they had spent the money from the sale of the pearls—what then?

Anna breathed a deep, shuddering sigh, responding to the bleak figures before her and the bitter cold that penetrated the room. She crumpled the paper and threw it into the fire. Gazing at the quickened flame, she slipped down before the hearth to savor the momentary heat and brightness. It was gone in an instant. She reached for the poker, banked the fire, turned back for her candle, and climbed the narrow stairs to bed.

Tiptoeing to the end of the icy passageway, Anna listened at the door of her sister's chamber. Often Lydia lay awake long into the night, and Anna would sit with her and hold her hand, both of them silent so as not to disturb Miss Bennet's sleep.

But tonight she could hear, beyond Miss Bennet's gentle snoring, the quiet, regular breathing of her sister. Anna turned with relief to her own bedchamber and closed the door behind her. The biting March wind found the candle flame and extinguished it without a sputter of protest. Anna shuddered, fumbled for the table, placed the candlestick on it, undressed with stiff fingers, and slipped between the frigid sheets. The hot brick Miss Bennet had used to warm her bed had long ago grown cold.

"Mr. Parrish would not give me even the meanest pickings until we had paid something on our account, my lady, so I thought I would ask Farmer Grubb for eggs. You know as well as I that he could help us if he had a mind to."

"Now, Benny, do not go 'my lady'-ing me, remember," Anna said, smiling to take the sting from her words. "Could you wait until tomorrow? I go to Mrs. Ives today."

"Of course . . . miss." Miss Maria Bennet, gaunt and stiff, of an age even Anna did not know, was quite aware that this was Anna's day to go to the Hall but as usual had allowed it to slip her mind. It happened every day Anna was due to sit with old Mrs. Ives as a paid companion. "Very well, I will go tomorrow, though it means Lydia will have to make do with gruel again."

"I will try to persuade Parrish to extend our credit."

Miss Bennet opened her mouth, but Anna, certain that only a lament would issue forth, gestured at the window and said, "It looks as though the storm has blown itself out and I shall have a pleasant drive after all."

"To think of you having to . . ."

"Is Lydie's milk ready? I will carry it in to her before I leave."

Miss Bennet abandoned her complaints to rush to prepare the milk, as Anna had known she would. She slipped from the kitchen before her former governess could rile herself over all the other offenses that tried her soul.

In the crowded sitting room Lydia lay on a worn sofa, gazing out the window. Anna watched her for a moment before making her presence known.

Lydia turned her head and smiled. "Do you have time to sit with me before you leave?"

"Of course." Anna sat down and picked up a book that had fallen from Lydia's grasp. "Cowper—I think I could have guessed."

"I was thinking of the line . . ." Lydia flushed and turned back to the window.

"What line?"

" 'With what intense desire she wants her home . . . ' " Lydia recited in a low voice.

Anna silently reached for her hand. Neither one looked at the other; each was alone with similar thoughts.

Bright sun streamed in and shone on the two faces, alike in many ways yet unhappily different in others. Both were beautiful with pale skin, delicate bones, and wide eyes. Lydia, however, was but moon to her sister's sun. Anna's hair was deep auburn and glowed like flame in the brilliant light. Her eyes were vivid green and her lips a deep red.

Lydia's hair was the color of flax, her eyes a shadowless blue, the pallor of her skin intensified by illness. She was sixteen, four years younger than her sister, but looked like a child. She had grown little in the last few years, not yet having filled a woman's form. To Anna it was as if Lydia's body required all the food she ate simply to keep her alive, sparing nothing that would allow her to grow and flourish. Not, she thought, that an invalid could flourish on the dreary sequence of meals that were Lydia's portion.

"I wish you did not have to go, Anna."

"Really, Lydie, I do not mind. I always hear or see something to amuse me at the Hall. And who knows, perhaps Cook will slip me something delicious today. That would be well worth a visit, wouldn't it?"

Lydia's face lit up.

Anna released her hand and leaned to kiss her. "Time to appease the dragon," she said with a laugh.

Lydia smiled, but her face fell into lines of loneliness and pain. Anna turned quickly and left the room.

Anna led the donkey from the shed behind the cottage to harness it to the cart. The donkey was nearly too old for these trips, but Anna knew the ground was too wet to walk the long miles to Lynthorpe Hall.

"Just remember the oats waiting for you, old dear," Anna said as she struggled to fasten the rough leather harness. Haste made her fumble awkwardly; she hurried, knowing that Miss Bennet would feel obliged to come to her aid. Miss Bennet, who had never adjusted to their having come down in the world, would sacrifice her last comfort to keep Anna from doing the rough labor that was now her lot.

Finally she pulled tight the last stiff strap, climbed up onto the narrow seat, and pulled into the rutted road that would take her to the Hall.

It was indeed clearing. The gray leaden clouds that had overhung the village for a fortnight were scudding toward the east, pushed by a cool wind that shook drops from the branches overhead. Despite the piercing cold, Anna thought she could smell the scent of earth awakening to spring. Her hopes began to rise.

She knew that Lydia and Miss Bennet pitied her these trips to Lynthorpe Hall, and she had not the heart to correct them, to tell them how gladly she anticipated the thrice-weekly trips to read to old Mrs. Ives and help her with her sewing. Mrs. Ives, the mother of the present squire, was too lively and intelligent to be anything but bored with her long days lost among her son's hunting-besotted family.

When the vicar had suggested to Mrs. Ives that she might like a companion, she had eagerly caught hold of the idea. And when the vicar in turn had recommended the plan to Anna, he had not confessed that he had conceived of it as a measure to swell Anna's slim purse. The arrangement had suited them both. The original day had expanded to three, and for Anna they were days of almost carefree pleasure.

Carefree pleasure! Once Anna would have laughed to think of a day passed in the company of an elderly lady, stitching and reading, as carefree pleasure. But they were pleasant days. Mrs. Ives was worldly and cheerful—sharing many of Anna's interests in literature. Best, perhaps, was the fact that she had a ready laugh and was unfailingly kind.

She was also quite generous. This day, for example, Anna wore a gift from Mrs. Ives, a grape wool gown of the softest merino and the silkiest warmth. Mrs. Ives had given the fabric to Anna in a fit of disgust with her extravagance at having purchased an entire bolt of such a very odd color. Anna had accepted it, undeceived, and fashioned gowns for the three of them at home. It was not a color she would have chosen, either, but she could not deny that it looked unusually well with her reddish hair.

Anna was most thankful for her wages. The fifteen shillings she earned would have been almost enough to support

them and their meager wants, were it not for the expense
of Lydia's medicines. Again Anna came to the same bleak
conclusion in her thoughts that she had in her figuring the
night before. Even with the value of the pearls, and her
wages and gifts from Mrs. Ives, they could not go on. They
would require more and more charity from neighbors and
shopkeepers already persuaded they had been charitable
enough. And nothing in the meanness of the penury she
foresaw would heal Lydia and make her strong.

Anna shook off her thoughts lest she begin to weep, the
only possible outcome of this line of thinking. On these
solitary trips, plying from the cottage to the Hall—the only
time she was ever alone—it was difficult not to become
bluedeviled.

She looked about her, deliberately opening her senses to
the signs of coming spring. From the top of a rise in the road
she thought she could discern green in a distant field. She
inhaled deeply and made an effort to relax her shoulders,
hunched against the cold, and she flexed her hands, aching
from a too-tight grip on the reins.

Anna gazed at the donkey and laughed. What a very
small thing it was, for all its strength and heart. She felt
a rush of affection for it as they started down the gentle rise and the donkey sped up with the release of the
weight.

Suddenly from behind came a terrifying roar of hooves,
and in a horrified backward glance Anna saw the wild
movement of galloping legs and tossing heads, the looming
height of a carriage and the churning of huge wheels. She
threw herself back, dragging at the reins, pulling with all
her might, crying for the donkey to turn into the bank.

The thundering chaos came upon her, and then, miraculously, it pulled away and passed on. In the instant the
vehicles were abreast, she caught a glimpse of furious
eyes in an angry face, of a gentleman whose grip on the
reins was almost as desperate as her own.

Anna collapsed in laughter. It was inexplicable and unlike her, but the instant the carriage had hurtled by and she knew she was safe from harm, she felt a rush of hilarity to think that such a fine gentleman had been inconvenienced by her poor old donkey cart.

His venom amused her as well. Did he think he owned the road? Of course he did, she thought with a sudden bitterness that she instantly reproved herself for. Making every effort to dismiss the driver from her mind, she continued on her way.

Despite her best intentions, from time to time she found herself smiling about the averted mishap and the arrogance of the large, dark man who had swept past her so majestically, in his mind—so foolishly in hers.

Anna drove the cart around to the stables where Jem waited to take charge of it. It might have seemed like a silly ritual to an onlooker, that her equipage should receive such attention, but it was typical of Mrs. Ives' kindness that Anna's humble donkey was to be sheltered in a warm stable and given the treat of good fodder while it waited for its mistress.

Anna scratched the donkey on the nose. "We had a wild ride this morning, didn't we, old thing? Were you as frightened as I?"

She smiled at Jem, and, turning away, she noticed the carriage, which she now saw was an ordinary curricle drawn by ordinary horses, albeit they were handsome matched bays. They were being led away by the groom for a rubbing-down—no doubt they would be in a fine lather, she thought with a smile, just like their master.

The smile lit her face, and the odd merriment that had possessed her since beholding the angry face of the mad driver who had almost run her over caused her to break into laughter.

She made her way from the paddock through the gardens to the near kitchen door, which swung open and revealed the man himself. Looming, arrogant, and very angry, he showed on his face that in encountering her he was encountering the very object of his venomous thoughts.

"You!" he said.

Anna paused and raised her eyebrows. "Are you speaking to me?"

"You are the wench in the donkey cart who tried to overset me just now, aren't you?"

Anna narrowed her eyes. "No."

"You cannot deny it."

Anna studied him. A head taller than she, dark, impeccably dressed, undoubtedly handsome but for his petulant expression, he was so used to getting his way that she decided in an instant to meet him insult for insult.

"It is amusing to be called a wench by a boor. And, yes, it was me on the public way, a right I believe every subject in our land possesses from birth. More deservedly, in truth, since I, unlike you, do not endanger the lives of others."

She stared defiantly into his angry and shocked face.

"Oh, no, you don't," he muttered as she tried to edge around him into the doorway.

She spun quickly and, eluding his grasp, ran into the kitchen, nearly colliding with one of the servants who was lugging a pan of water to empty in the yard.

From within a dark passage Anna rose to her toes and looked through a grimy window. She could almost read his thoughts as he stared first at the kitchen door, then at the maid, and back at the door. She watched his face assume what was no doubt its habitual haughty expression before he turned on his heel and strode back to the stables. A squabble with a servant, Anna guessed, was far beneath his dignity.

She laughed and executed a profound curtsy. *Your peacock majesty!* she thought and, still laughing, stood aside for the maid, who looked at her in astonishment.

Chapter
Two

ANNA GREETED THE kitchen staff with more than her customary good humor. Mrs. Whitaker, the cook, looked at her curiously, but Anna offered no explanations as she undid her cloak, untied her bonnet, and put them tidily away under a bench as was her custom.

"A fine day!" she said.

"Indeed it is, and you're in fine looks yourself!" Mrs. Whitaker responded.

"What is this?" Anna exclaimed, bending over a fragrant confection cooling on the long, white central table.

"Molasses cake. Do you have time to try some?"

Anna laughed. "This kitchen is magic! It happens every time I enter through that door that some cake or pudding has miraculously just emerged from the oven. How is that, do you think?"

"I wouldn't know," Mrs. Whitaker replied. "The oven must like you. How is Lydia doing today?"

"Better, I think. I am hoping with the spring she will be

able to venture out. It is not long until spring, you know."

"I know, dear." Mrs. Whitaker touched Anna's arm briefly as she laid a slice of cake and a cup of tea on the table.

Returning to her tasks, Mrs. Whitaker spoke to divert Anna's mind from the contemplation of her sister's health which she knew occupied her all too often. "The squire is hosting a meeting of the hunt to decide whether or not to join with the Blues, another hunt group. We have folks arriving today, and we are just about walked off our feet with the cooking."

"Ah! I think I might have encountered one on the road."

"To be sure. They have been arriving all morning. Some are still in the library, although most have gone off riding, even with the ground being as wet as it is."

"I wonder if Mrs. Ives is with them . . . in the library, I mean. She may have forgotten to tell me not to come."

"Oh, she's waiting for you—you know she can't stand anything having to do with horses. Mrs. Harry Ives is riding, I know, and the squire wants to be, although I think he is stuck at the house greeting latecomers."

"Poor Mrs. Ives. How did she end up with such a family?"

"I'm sure she has asked herself that many times."

Anna swallowed the last of her tea, and rose. "I had better go to her, then. She is probably staying in her room to avoid them and longing for some company."

"Stop by on your way home, and we'll see if there might not be something for you to take back to Lydia."

"Oh, Mrs. Whitaker, you are kind. I do not know what we would do without your help."

"It's nothing, dear. Even if the master knew, I don't think he would begrudge it. But since he doesn't—what he doesn't know won't hurt him, will it?"

Anna winced at the implied conspiracy to defraud the squire, but since she was perfectly willing to beg for the food Mrs. Whitaker gave her, she was only grateful that it was never necessary. She touched the cook's hand in gratitude and left the dark and cavernous kitchen to make her way through the narrow passageways to the back stairs and Mrs. Ives' room.

The second flight of stairs gave onto a green baize-covered door that led to the front of the house through a wide hallway interrupted by deeply recessed, dark wood doors. Anna knocked at the fourth one and waited until Mrs. Ives bade her enter.

After an interval during which she waited vainly for a response, she pushed the heavy door open and stepped into a room swathed in crimson damask and crowded with furniture that its occupant had squirreled from other rooms in the house.

Mrs. Ives sat on a chaise near the fire. She eagerly leaned toward someone with whom she was speaking. Anna could see only the back of a head above a tall chair, a leg ending in a gleaming boot, and a strong hand holding an impossibly delicate teacup. She needed no more to know that it was the nemesis of the morning's ride intruding into her life yet again.

She let the door close loudly so that the two who had not noticed her entrance could not fail to notice it now.

Mrs. Ives lifted her head and peered into the gloomy shadows made by the draperies before the door.

"Anna, my dear," she said kindly, "do come in. I have a friend I would like you to meet."

Anna walked directly to the chaise and made a show of greeting Mrs. Ives with exclamations and hugs, as though oblivious to the presence of anyone in the wing chair. In her warmest and most melodic voice, she said, "Dear Mrs. Ives, how lovely you look!"

"Thank you, dear. You are in high color today." Sophia Ives leaned forward, the drapings of lace on her head and shoulders fluttering about her. She gestured to the wing chair. "But here, I would like you to meet . . ."

"Ma'am, did I tell you that Maria Wentworth sends her love?" the man asked in a slow drawl. "I saw her and Harold last month in Berkshire."

Anna did not turn to the man whose exclusive conversation with his hostess was certainly intended to snub her. Mrs. Ives held her by the hand, and trapped, Anna kept her gaze earnestly fixed on her.

Mrs. Ives turned eagerly. "Maria Rees, that was. How is she? You know, your mother could never stomach her."

"Whom could my mother stomach but you?" He spoke diffidently, Anna thought, nearly yawning in counterfeit ease.

"Come, she was not as impossible as all that, although to be sure, she had a sharp tongue. But you must allow me to . . ."

Anna could have felt foolish being forced to stand like a statue overlooked by the one, stroked and worried over by the other. But she found a certain relish in the game.

"No sharper than yours, she would have argued. 'The Serpent Sophia' she used to call you."

Mrs. Ives laughed. "I like that! But rusticating in Yorkshire has dulled me, I am afraid. But, Horace, you must permit me to introduce my friend."

Deciding to intensify the game, Anna turned away. Speaking softly over her shoulder, she said, "But I waste my time in idle conversation when I should be about my work. I have not yet completed the hem of the overskirt on your gray gown."

She crossed to a table in a dim corner, opened a large chest, and took from it the gown. She unrolled it and elaborately inspected the work she had done, intent and rapt, seemingly lost in thought.

Out of the corner of her eye, she saw that the man had reluctantly stood when Mrs. Ives had essayed her last introduction and was now the one to stand awkwardly waiting for an acknowledgment Anna was much too absorbed to grant. He sat back down abruptly, leaving Mrs. Ives looking bewildered.

A stab of remorse for using her friend as a pawn in a silly game impelled Anna to return to them. Ignoring him still, she selected a chair near his, but instead of sitting so that she could see and be seen by him, she acted a charade of shifting about so as to obtain the very best light, and turned ever so slightly so that her back was fully to him.

Mrs. Ives tried again. "Horace, I would like to present Anna Smith. Horace is the son of a dear friend of mine from Lincolnshire—I do miss Vinny," she said with a sigh. "—Horace Crewe, Baron of Trent."

Anna made a great show of attempting to rise, to gather up the voluminous gown so that it would not brush the floor, to secure the needle so that it would not become lost, and yet managed, despite her best efforts, to drop the scissors coincidentally with his giving her what appeared to be, out of the corner of her eye, a splendid leg. Finally she succeeded in rising to her feet, bobbing a clumsy curtsy, and mumbling a response so apparently abashed and humble that he could never have heard it. She was delighted to discover, as she lifted her face to the light to thread the needle, after regaining her seat, that his lips were pursed in anger and his cheeks bore the telltale tinge of choler.

Their puzzled hostess looked from one to the other. She arranged the folds of her elaborate fichu and settled her cap on her gray curls. "Horace has been so good as to visit me, even though I am quite certain that he would much rather be riding with the others. He is a fine whip, you see, quite famous. Rumor has it that he once drove from Bath to Cheltenham in just under three hours!"

"Oh, dear," said Anna, "how alarming! Imagine, ma'am, all the people he must have run off the road to achieve that!"

"Fancy your saying that! Just this morning he had a terrible experience. He was almost overset by—what did you say?—anyway, a bumpkin in a cart that blocked the entire road."

After a silence which Crewe was evidently not planning to fill, Anna said demurely, "What a dreadful experience for a whip! What could be done about that, do you think? Perhaps an outrider of some sort running ahead, crying, 'Make way, make way for a fine whip, make way!'"

Mrs. Ives laughed but looked a little confused.

Crewe spoke. "Mrs. Ives exaggerates my complaint. I merely said that I had had an annoying episode on the road this morning."

"Why, Horace, that is not at all what you said. You said that—I know! 'Some vulgar shrew with more hair than wit' halted her cart on the slope of a hill where you could not possibly have seen it. Yes, I am sure that is what you said—'a vulgar shrew with more hair than wit.'"

"I may have said that, ma'am, but no doubt it was only exaggeration for poetic effect."

Anna, not taking her eyes from her industrious needle, said, "One so seldom has a chance to meet a man with the reckless daring of a fine whip united with the sensitivity of a poet. Is that not so in your opinion, ma'am?"

"I say, Horace would surprise you! He has many arrows in his quiver, many talents indeed. We were only now talking about one . . . is it a secret, Horace? Could I tell Anna what we were discussing?"

"I cannot suppose that I have any secrets that would entertain Miss Smith."

Anna smiled into her stitches.

"Horace saw Wellesley! Met with him! He worked with Peterson at the Foreign Office and was sent to Ligny with a dispatch the night before the battle of Waterloo and had a private audience with him."

Interested despite herself, Anna merely replied, "Indeed! One always assumes that Wellington is a handsome man.

Is that your guess, too, ma'am, that he is uncommonly handsome?"

"Horace, what would you say to that?"

"I would not hazard a guess on a question that certainly ought only to be judged by ladies. For myself, I was looking for other qualities. I found him, for instance, to be intelligent, bold, and remarkably courteous."

"How gratified the duke would be, my lord," Anna responded, "to hear your opinion. What a shame that he is denied it."

"Why, I think Wellesley is generally accounted intelligent," Mrs. Ives said, a bit doubtfully.

"Only to the perceptive, I believe," Anna, leaning toward her, said in a mock whisper.

Another silence fell. Anna hid her smile by turning toward the windows and seeking out a sign of sunlight between the thick draperies.

"It is a shame that George is not here," Mrs. Ives said, attempting to test another topic. "We expect him for the long vacation, of course, but when he gets away he is far more likely to be off with friends from Balliol than to languish here."

"I miss him. He is the only one in the family, present company excepted, of course, who can speak of anything but foxes, hounds, and bruising riding."

"Yes, he is the best of the lot. Why my son and his wife were able to produce only one sensible child between them, I am sure I cannot say."

"Are his studies going well?"

"He is a bright lad. Favors me, of course."

Anna and the baron laughed.

"What are you reading these days?"

"Whatever this dear child chooses to read to me. I am quite in her hands. Lately it has been the most insipid effort by Maria Edgeworth."

"Are you thoroughly at her mercy, then?"

"No, Horace. Anna is no ogre. We have our special way of reading Miss Edgeworth, do we not, Anna?"

Anna lifted her face, her eyes bright with laughter. While Horace could not discern her features, silhouetted as she was against the lamplight, he saw the conspiring look pass between them.

"What special way is that?" he asked warily.

"Oh, you may inquire, but I doubt that Anna will satisfy you."

"If it lies in Miss Smith's hands, then I would not look for satisfaction."

"No," Mrs. Ives continued, oblivious, unlike Anna, to the sting of the remark. "I do not think so, either. Anna, I cannot hope that you would favor us with your very particular rendition of Miss Edgeworth . . ."

"Not today, ma'am. I believe that kind of frivolous occupation is best kept to ourselves."

Mrs. Ives laughed. "You see, we have such contempt for Miss Edgeworth's heroine that Anna fell to reading her speeches in a mincing, whining voice that makes every word she utters ridiculous. And she has given the villain a preposterous accent that makes his most ferocious speeches downright ludicrous. We do have a gay time . . ."

Anna hated herself for the blush she felt on her cheeks. She did not give a fig what this popinjay thought of her humorous starts.

"How fortunate you are to have the efforts of a celebrated authoress at the mercy of your fine wit."

It was the first remark Crewe had addressed directly to Anna, and she was forming her response when Mrs. Ives burst out indignantly, "Horace, you must not defend Maria Edgeworth unless you have read her, which I am quite sure you have not. Have you?"

"I have not had that pleasure, no."

"Then hush."

Anna laughed outright and glanced at Crewe to see him

make the effort to quell a blush with a haughty sneer. She hastily looked away and worked the needle intently.

His next conversational effort was clearly meant to exact revenge. "Miss Smith. Smith. I do not believe I know a Smith among the members of the Aldenbury Hunt. Does your father ride?"

Anna replied stiffly. "My father is dead."

"I am so sorry. Was he a member of the hunt?"

Anna wanted to say what her father would have thought of the Aldenbury Hunt, but limited herself to a curt, "No, my lord."

"It is so unusual for a County family not to be a member of the hunt. Was your father opposed to blood sports?"

Mrs. Ives intervened. "I am opposed to blood sports in any form, Horace," she said with a meaningful glance at Anna. Despite her own curiosity about the reasons for the disparity between Anna's present circumstance and the station in life she had once occupied, she felt protective enough to cease her own efforts to discover Anna's story and to shield her from the tactlessness of others.

"Ma'am," said Horace, acknowledging defeat.

There was another silence through which Anna stitched purposefully.

"Will you be going to London in the summer, Horace?"

"Perhaps, although George and I were talking about the possibility of a journey to Paris now that the war is over. Has he mentioned anything of this to you?"

"You assume he writes! You know George—I have not seen him since Christmas, and at that time he did not mention it."

"No matter, some new freak will have caught his attention by then. Well, ma'am, I must pay my respects to the squire, although I hate to abandon the pleasures of your company."

"Yes, you must. He is very puffed up about the possibility of your joining the hunt."

"I am fortunate to have such a distinguished hunt in the vicinity of my father's lodge."

" 'Distinguished hunt'—what codswallop, Horace!"

Laughing, Crewe stood to take his leave from Mrs. Ives.

Anna studied him as, with his back to her, he said his good-byes. He was a fine-looking man, she concluded unwillingly. Dressed soberly, in a dark blue coat and doeskin breeches, he displayed vanity in the very high polish of his boots and the immaculateness of every garment. His hair was black, long and thick, worn in careless curls, or rather, she thought contemptuously, as careless as three hairdressers working over him every morning could make them.

The contempt in her face surprised Crewe, who turned at that moment to sketch a bow. She eyed him coolly and surrendered the barest courtesy she could without being completely rude. And then he was gone.

Chapter Three

AS THE DOOR closed behind Lord Crewe, Mrs. Ives turned to Anna with a frown.

"I cannot imagine what possessed Horace today. Ordinarily he is the most affable of men. It is unlike him to be high in the instep. And you, my dear, have been quiet. Are you not in spirits? How is Lydia today?"

"She is much the same, thank you, ma'am. As for myself, I am very well, thank you, and I thought Lord Crewe quite charming."

"Nonsense, girl. You did no such thing." Mrs. Ives rose from the chaise and adjusted her skirts. "Is it not odd how, when you get two people together whom you are sure will like each other—because you especially like them—they so often take an instant dislike to each other?"

"You quite exaggerate, Mrs. Ives. I took no dislike to the baron and I certainly hope I gave him no cause to dislike me."

"No, my dear, I never meant to suggest that he did. La!

Is that clock right? Can it be past noon already? Would you ring for Alice to bring my dinner early? I am going to have to fortify myself with a longer nap than usual if I am to get through one of John's interminable evenings."

Anna, smiling, went to the thick red cord and gave it a tug, then returned to her chair, where she shook out the work she had completed and offered it up to Mrs. Ives' inspection.

"You do very nice work, Anna. I can see that you were as patient at your needlework as you were at your studies. You must have been quite a satisfactory pupil in all things." It was a modest ploy, and, as usual, Anna met the invitation to discuss her past with a polite smile and complete silence.

There was a knock on the door, and a maid whom Anna did not know entered bearing a tray of food for the two of them. Anna assumed that Alice, Mrs. Ives' usual maid, had been pressed into service for the large gathering below.

After having leisurely partaken of their meal, Mrs. Ives rang for the maid to prepare her for bed, apologizing to Anna for cutting short their time together. "I feel quite sorry for myself. I admit—I would love to hear you read a few more chapters of la Maria, but I must rest if I am to have any patience with the imbeciles tonight."

"I understand, ma'am. I only hope you can contrive to enjoy yourself a little."

"I am sure I shan't."

The two women laughed and embraced, and Anna quietly let herself out of the room.

It was hours earlier than she usually finished for the day, and the sudden freedom meant returning to the baleful company of Miss Bennet. Perhaps she could arrange a special treat for Lydia—although the unlooked-for hours themselves would be treat enough. She could not return, however, until she found Alice, Mrs. Ives' maid, and secured her wages. It was imperative to pay something on the butcher's bill tomorrow.

Hoping to find her, she made her way to the kitchen.

The kitchen was Bedlam with dishes being returned to the scullery from the dining room above, additional platters and serving bowls being borne upstairs, and in the middle of it all, harried and hot, her cap askew on her perspiring brow, was Mrs. Whitaker. Anna backed out quietly—it was certainly no time to bother her.

She was in a quandary—she must wait, but there was no place to wait, as she did not have the freedom of the house. Anna thought it best to retreat to the out-of-doors and enjoy the opportunity to stroll on the gravel paths until the confusion in the kitchens subsided and the servants were free.

Anna stepped out into the bright sunshine and strolled through the shrubbery. She had not retrieved her cloak or bonnet, but the sun was warm and the wind calm, and the high hedges sheltered her. She gazed about her at the tips of green pushing up through the earth and the path of crocuses flowing beyond the enclosure. The windows at the back of the house were busy with passing figures, and Anna realized that it must be the dining room overlooking her path and was reminded of the Baron of Trent.

At that instant, as though summoned by her thoughts, Crewe stepped out through a pair of tall glass doors. On his arm was a beautiful woman attired in a tartan habit of a cut and design Anna could only assume was exquisitely fashionable, with her blond hair swept up under a plumed bonnet.

She watched them descend from the terraces, ambling down a path toward the stables away from her. The woman lifted her face to Crewe, who bent toward her and spoke into her ear. As they straightened, the breeze carried the sound of their laughter to Anna.

Slowly she turned back to the kitchen. The meal must have ended, then, and she would be able to find Alice and return home.

The last of the dishes were being returned for washing, and the maids were untying their serving aprons and donning the plainer ones they wore in the kitchen. Anna scanned the faces but could not find Alice. Mrs. Whitaker was not to be seen, either.

As she stood in the doorway, undecided and awkward, Hawkins, the footman who waited table and whom Mrs. Ives considered a pretentious and supercilious fool—an opinion Anna had no reason to refute—bore down upon her.

"If it's handouts you're wanting today, you won't get any. Mrs. Whitaker is resting in the servants' hall, so you'll just have to go home empty-handed today."

Anna longed to slap the smugness off his face. She mustered up the most humble politeness and asked, "Do you know where Alice is?"

"Yes, I know where Alice is."

"Where is she, please."

"She's with her mam. Her mam's ailing in Woford, and she's gone to take care of her. There'll be no charity for you today, it looks like."

Anna stepped away from him as from a foul odor. Turning, she retreated to the hallway. What should she do? With Alice gone, she would have to wait for Mrs. Ives to awaken and secure her wages from her directly—that might be hours, and she hated to face the prospect of returning home in the dark. She could not, in fact—it was simply not safe to do so. She would have to come for them tomorrow.

Anna pressed her fingers to her temples. She had counted on the money to pay Parrish tomorrow. She had counted on—yes—charity from Mrs. Whitaker. To go home empty-handed!

She paced up and down the passageway, but the scurrying of the servants made her aware that she was in the way and had no business there. Betsy, one of the upstairs

maids, bumped into her, balancing a tray of glasses on
her upturned palm. She recoiled, struggling to regain her
balance, and they both stood with eyes widened in horror
as the glasses gradually stopped trembling.

"Cor, that was close!" Betsy said.

"Oh, Betsy. I am sorry—I seem to be in the way. Betsy,"
she asked, stretching out her hand, "do you know when Mrs.
Ives might be done with her nap?"

"I didn't even know you weren't with her. Everything's
all a muddle. One of the gentlemen has gone and lost
something—a stickpin, I think, and I'm supposed to be
looking for it, but I can't until I put the silver away.
Maybe you wouldn't mind helping. Anderson would be
that grateful, I know he would. He has a soft spot for you,
thinks you're the model for all us maids—not that you're a
maid, of course. It's in the library—he's supposed to have
lost it in the library. Would you mind looking?"

Anna, looking into the cheerful, open countenance before
her, knew Betsy could never understand how painful Anna
found her words. Betsy took her silence as an affirmative.

"Oh, thanks. If it's not in the library, he says perhaps
the dining room, although they've already searched there.
It could even be upstairs, but the housekeeper is looking
there."

"I will search in the library, then. A stickpin, did you say?
Do you know what color or how big it is?"

"That I don't, miss, but it's very fine and very valuable,
to hear Anderson tell it. He's that worried about it, he is.
Doesn't want any of the guests to go away saying things
disappear at Lynthorpe Hall!"

"No, indeed."

Anna climbed the stairs to the first story and walked
along the brightly lit hall to the library. It was mercifully
empty. She had dreaded, although she just now realized it,
running into the baron and his companion.

Standing just within the doorway, she looked about without moving forward, dismayed that such a small thing would never show itself easily. Against a Turkish carpet with a busy pattern it would be difficult to distinguish anything. She did see a sherry glass lying under a chair and picked it up and sniffed. She remembered the lovely fragrance of her father's sherry. She tilted her head and reminiscently breathed in the smell again.

Lost in dreams and memory, gazing unseeing before her, she let the pungent smell lead her into the past. Suddenly she frowned and focused on the carpet where she had been absently staring.

For a moment she thought it was a trick of light, but she moved her head and she saw it still—something gleaming against a leg of the heavy table that occupied the center of the room.

She had found it! She was astonished that it had been so easy. Placing the glass on the table, she bent and lifted it off the carpet.

It was a stickpin for a cravat, she thought, a short sharp pin having lost its guard. She held it in the palm of her hand and turned it to see the design.

Her eyebrows shot up. "Goodness," she said aloud. Could these really be emeralds and rubies? she wondered, looking at a design of green and red stones forming concentric circles around a central gold dome. If they were, she could not even begin to imagine its value.

She gazed at it, fascinated. How little it was. No wonder it had been lost.

She straightened and tightened her fist around it. She would find Anderson and turn it over to him. When she did, she would mention to him that with Alice gone, she had not received her wages. Perhaps he would pay her out of household money, grateful to have the jewel recovered and the crisis averted.

She opened her fist again and studied the design. Perhaps eight rubies, ten emeralds. None of them very big—about the size of the petals on her mother's daisy brooch. But undoubtedly valuable . . .

Footsteps in the hall startled her, and she turned hastily to leave before whoever it was should enter.

At the door she collided with Lord Crewe. She gasped, frozen, and could only stare.

Horace Crewe stared back. Her beauty took his breath away. He had not truly seen her before without the shadows of her bonnet. Mrs. Ives' darkened room had obscured her features. She was all brightness—glowing hair, bright eyes, red lips . . .

Anna observed his scrutiny of her as it changed from a stranger's regard of another stranger to a man's regard of a woman.

After a long moment she remembered herself, sketched a curtsy, tucked her head to hide from his gaze, and edged by him to make her escape.

Without meaning to, Crewe reached out his hand and touched her arm. "Wait."

She backed away, still looking at him, then turned and fled down the hall.

When she got to the stairs, she paused behind the door and tried to catch her breath.

Why had she behaved like a ninnyhammer? She lifted her hands to her burning cheeks and was recalled to the presence of the jewel clenched in her fist. Leaning against the door she opened her hand and looked at the stickpin in the dim light. Then, quite slowly, she took her handkerchief from the pocket deep in her skirt, unfolded it, laid the jewel in it, wrapped it carefully, and returned it to her pocket.

She stared at the wall opposite, took a deep breath, and admitted what she already knew. She was going to keep it. She could not account for the decision. Perhaps she had meant to from the moment she had seen it. Perhaps it had something to do with having seen Crewe. But she would never relinquish it. It was hers.

Collectedly, as though she had not stolen another's property, she descended the stairs and walked through the hall into the kitchen. When Betsy turned inquiringly to her, she lifted her shoulders. "I was unable to find it, but I was interrupted when one of the gentlemen came into the library. You will need to search it later."

"Don't worry, I'll go as soon as I'm done here. But it'll never be found, mark my words. A stickpin! Just as soon look for a needle in a haystack, if you ask me."

"You are probably right, Betsy."

Jem had yet to hitch the donkey to the cart, Anna having come early from the Hall, and while she waited she thought to herself, *I am not going home with wages, nor with a quarter of a shepherd's pie, nor a crock of milk with the rich cream floating on top, nor a mutton shank with meat still clinging to it. I am returning with something that will take us to the healing waters in Bath.*

In the little cottage under the close-growing larches, the atmosphere that evening differed in a way that only Anna understood. Lydia eagerly anticipated her sister's return and the surprises she might bring with her. Disappointment that she had returned empty-handed was not a part of their evening, for Anna was merry, and the merriment was infectious.

Lydia lay and watched her sister bustle about, preparing their tea, which they took at a table brought up between the sofa and the fire. Their meal consisted of a thin soup flavored faintly by an already overboiled bone and the last of the swedes from the autumn's harvest of their garden. As usual, the most generous helping with the only appetizing bits of vegetable had been ladled into Lydia's bowl.

The bread they used to soak up the last of the broth from the pot had been baked the previous week by Anna. Miss Bennet had originally undertaken to do the baking, as she had intended to shoulder all the domestic tasks, but it had, of course, proved far too much for her. Besides, as she had grudgingly admitted, Anna had a way with bread that was almost shameful to a lady born.

The dab of butter left from an earlier gift of Mrs. Whitaker found its way to Lydia's slice, neither Miss Bennet nor Anna feeling inclined to so much richness.

Lydia saw through the subterfuge but did not protest. It was her duty to get well, and they all knew that she must eat everything that came her way if she were to do so. Oh, how she wished she could get well by drawing, or reading, or admiring Anna and sitting laughing and talking with her. For those were the things that brought her joy, since her adoration of her older sister was deep and thorough. But eating! She was never ready to eat; meals came too soon again for her, and always with the kinds of food she found most difficult: greasy soups, heavy butter, and dense breads.

Lydia thought back to the food she remembered from childhood, to the fruit especially. How she would love an orange. Or a peach! How long had it been since she had eaten . . . She looked guiltily at Anna. If she knew how ungrateful she was— *Poor Anna*, she thought, *she works so hard, and all I can do is dream of oranges and peaches!*

"This is such good bread, Annie, and what a treat to have butter!"

Anna answered her with a roguish smile. *Really*, thought Lydia, *Anna is quite different tonight.*

"Butter! Just you wait, my Lydie, someday we shall have so much butter that we spread it on our cheeks for perfect skins and heap it on the hearth just to enjoy the spectacle of watching it melt."

Miss Bennet shook her head in stiff disapproval.

"The idea of butter to excess has a certain appeal, Annie," Lydia said, "but could we try something more exotic? Bananas, perhaps?"

"But bananas do not melt," said Anna, chewing her bread thoughtfully. "The point is both excess and wastefulness."

"Well, could we not have bananas, huge heaps of them, and well, give them away, maybe, or hang them from the trees for decoration?"

"Float them down the river," Anna added. "Little yellow barges."

Lydia laughed. "Tell me more about the awful Lord Crewe."

Anna had, as usual, transformed her experiences at the Hall into the kind of amusing and interesting incident that would alleviate her sister's boredom. She had described the fatuous Hawkins and Mrs. Ives' outspoken disdain for her son's hunting, but had embroidered most upon the character of Lord Crewe. From the near escape with her life on the road to his pompous manner in conversation, she had described—complete with gestures and accent—all her encounters with him, all but the last, in the library with the jewel in her hand and his eyes fixed on hers.

Lydia giggled at the image of his pointless pride, and even Miss Bennet had been forced to smile, despite trying valiantly not to do so. She felt it her duty to be a sobering influence on the girls. But it was hard to resist her precious Anna when she was laughing with flushed cheeks and sparkling eyes.

As they sipped their weak tea, brewed from leaves that had been first pressed into service days ago, they fell into reverie. Lydia thought how good it would be to have Anna with her tomorrow for an entire day of reading and talking. The vicar, who often tried to visit when Lydia was alone, had made the loan of a book Lydia was saving as a surprise for Anna.

Miss Bennet was glad that Anna would not be going to the Hall, for it hurt her pride as nothing else did that her darling girl should be the paid companion of a common woman like Mrs. Ives. Her darling—the daughter of an earl!

But she struggled to suppress her thoughts, knowing that she was inclined to bitterness and that bitterness unchecked could poison the lives of all of them in the tiny cottage.

Odd, she thought to herself, that she felt so much more bitterness than either Anna or Lydia. She believed that she missed the privileges and comforts they had long ago left behind far more than the girls did.

Anna's thoughts were markedly different from those of her companions, and had her sister and former governess known them, they would have been shocked to their toes.

Her mind was churning with plans for the future based on the tiny chips of shiny stones that still resided in a square of white lawn in the pocket against her leg. Between each commonplace remark, each silly exchange, she dreamed of Bath's salubrious waters and of their healing effect on Lydia.

She leaned back in her chair, cradling her cup in her hands, and gazed at the fire. She indulged in the fantasy she had secretly nurtured ever since Lydia had become so terrifyingly unwell—Anna was sure—from living in penury in this dank, dark cottage. They would be in Bath. Lydia would drink a glass of the magic waters. She would sip, and take another sip. Suddenly she would be well! Her body would grow rounded and strong, her color would return, energy and strength would run through her veins, and she would leap up and dance through the crowds, springing with health and joy.

"What are you smiling about, Annie?" Lydia asked. "Something else that happened today?"

"Just dreaming. Wondering what it would be like to travel—to see places like Bath or London . . ."

Miss Bennet cleared her throat and looked frowningly at Anna. They fell silent. For the second time that night Anna had violated the rule they had established from the beginning—never to refer to what they had lost but to concentrate on the obtainable pleasures at hand.

She changed the subject to describe the meal she had seen served at the Hall while thinking with satisfaction that soon they would have bountiful meals, trips to warm and pleasant places, and that Lydia would be restored to health.

Chapter
Four

LATER THAT NIGHT, long after she was certain that
Lydia and Miss Bennet were asleep, Anna lit a candle in
her cold chamber and withdrew the handkerchief from its
hiding place. She shook it open and, in cold panic, at first
could not locate the stickpin. But it was there. She lifted it to
the flame. The stones were beautifully faceted, glittering in
the unsteady light of her candle. Again she wondered what
they were worth. Miss Bennet might have hazarded a guess,
for she had sold Anna's jewels when they had first come
here five years ago, before Anna had grown old enough to
take over the household affairs.

But Miss Bennet would never guess, for she would never
know about it. Anna would go with Farmer Grubb the next
time he drove to York for market day, and arrange to sell
one of the stones. Or two. Only when she knew how much
money they would have would she be able to lay her plans.

She rose from the bed and took down the oaken box that
had held her mother's most precious possessions; but now

the only jewel that lay against its velvet interior was the pearl pendant, wrapped in a bit of satin cloth, that had been her father's gift for her fourteenth birthday. She laid the stickpin in the box under a pile of mementos from their old home. She replaced the box above the old clothespress, changed into her bedgown, and slipped into bed.

She snuggled down to the middle of the bed, tucking the covers around her shoulders, and closed her eyes for sleep, but they sprang open. *What if I could get twenty pounds?* she wondered. *Thirty? That would surely be enough to get us to Bath.* Bath was not the only spa, of course, there was Clifton—but Bath was famous for its waters. And it was also where her grandmother lived.

Anna shuddered. Her grandmother had never forgiven her son for his marriage to the sixth daughter of an impoverished vicar, accomplished and beautiful as Louisa had been. After her son's death, she had found no reason to interest herself in the orphaned girls she had never met. Phrases from her grandmother's letter would be with her forever: "Never expect a shilling . . . your mother's profligacy and extravagance . . . debts . . . your father's honor . . . driven to the grave . . ."

It was a tissue of lies about her mother, but it did not matter how graceful and beautiful her mother had been. It was because her father had killed himself that his mother would never forgive them.

That is, forgive any of them but Lydia. Lydia, with her golden hair and enormous blue eyes, was the perfect image of her father. The same chiseled features, the same Roman lips. Her grandmother could not know this, never having seen her son's children. But surely, were she to see Lydia, her heart would melt. . . .

Anna turned restlessly, calling herself a fool for believing that one glimpse of Lydia would cause their grandmother to take them in and give them the family they so desperately needed. . . .

But it was a night to dream of drastic solutions, and so she allowed herself to dream about Bath.

And of a man's eyes changing from surprise to awareness . . .

She poked at the pillow and shifted her position again. "The coxcomb!"

Anna awoke with the same energy that had imbued her actions the evening before, and it was contagious. The small cottage was alive with cheerfulness and song as she kneaded dough for bread and glanced at the handful of barley she was hoping would swell enough to serve as filling for another soup. By midmorning she had finished what few meal preparations their meager larder allowed and eagerly went to sit with Lydia. Miss Bennet had assigned her a page of Latin to translate, and after she had talked with her about it, they read together from the new novel by Mme. d'Arblay which the vicar had brought.

But she could no longer put off the trip she must make to the village. Indeed, all visits to the village shops were painful for Anna, and she far too often left it to Miss Bennet to haggle and plead and try to wring the necessary goods from them while paying with promises. This morning it would be easier, for she had decided to use a few of the remaining shillings toward her bills there. She could afford such largess now, with the jewels tucked safely away.

Setting her bonnet on her head, her cloak over her shoulders, and the pattens onto her boots to keep them out of the mire of the rutted road, she set off for the village. It was a two-mile walk, and everywhere Anna discerned signs of advancing spring. There seemed no doubt that even here in the far reaches of the north of England, spring was determined to break through. The antics of the squirrels and the busy fluttering and hopping of the birds made them seem to be glorying in the absence of snow beneath their feet.

The sudden sound of a carriage coming up rapidly behind her caused her to jerk her head around and her heart to beat wildly. But it was only the apothecary. She waved to him and tried to persuade herself that her reaction had only been due to fear of being run down.

She arrived in the village and passed the smithy whence poured forth billows of smoke. She craned her head to see if the establishment were burning down, but the hazy figures she discerned within seemed remarkably unconcerned about the amount of smoke.

Her eyes were still stinging as she made her way to the nearly empty butcher's shop. Most of the women in the village had come and gone, which was not at all accidental. *When you buy on tick,* Anna thought, *you make your rounds when the shops are empty.*

Mr. Parrish greeted her with a formal courtesy at odds with his blood-spattered smock and disgusting hands. He happily carried out his butchering in full view of the customers, and Anna had been forced to perfect stern control to endure the trial of having to watch her selection of meat hacked from a carcass before her eyes.

"Good day, Miss Smith, and how are Miss Lydia and Miss Bennet?"

"Very well, thank you, Mr. Parrish. And I hope that Mrs. Parrish and Master Parrish, Miss Parrish and Sally, Flora, Timothy, and Jane are well, too."

Mr. Parrish smiled, gratified at hearing the imposing list of his progeny. "They are fine, thank you, Miss Smith. Lovely day—it's spring, don't you think?"

"It is, indeed."

And so the conversation proceeded through the ritual inquiries and pronouncements until it was fitting for Anna to broach the subject of her visit regretfully, as though sorry it was not the social call they would both have preferred.

"I believe it is time for us to pay something toward our account. You have been kind enough to extend credit, and we must not take advantage of you. Here," she said, handing over the coins, "would you please apply this against our debt to you?"

The butcher was surprised but gracefully concealed it. "Thank you, Miss Smith. I value your custom."

"Thank you, Mr. Parrish. Well, to celebrate, I think I will take some beef. A shin bone with some meat on it, but not too dear."

"What are you celebrating, if I may ask?"

She was celebrating the purchase of some real meat, but she spread her hands and said, "Why, spring, of course!"

Mr. Parrish laughed as he rooted around on a shelf for a good, meaty bone. "Spring has a lot to answer for, though. You heard about the trouble up at the Hall, I suppose."

"Trouble at the Hall?" Anna asked.

He did not answer directly but frowned at two bones, trying to take the measure of the meat left on them.

Anna turned away, feeling apprehension, and wondered at the prospect of learning unsettling news from a man covered in pigs' entrails.

He looked up and wiped his hands on the unspeakable cloth tied around his ample girth. "Well, seems like they've had a theft there, and they've been questioning the staff. Everything is at sixes and sevens."

"Theft?" Anna put her hand to her throat.

"Some lord staying there. Says he lost a ring with a diamond as big as an egg. So they've had the girls by the heels. Probably dismiss all the awkward and foolish maids as a way to get rid of them, and no doubt it will turn up in his pocket where he forgot he put it." Mr. Parrish's contempt for the gentry was widely known; in fact, it was even suspected that he had had sympathy for Bounaparte.

It must be the stickpin he was talking about. Theft? How could they know? But they could not know she had taken it. Could they? Surely she was safe. But . . .

" . . . be enough?"

Anna blinked and looked at Mr. Parrish, who seemed to be speaking from a vast echoing distance. She felt dizzy.

"Are you all right, miss?"

"Certainly. I am fine, Mr. Parrish."

"Here's your bone, but you know," he said suddenly, "I think I've got something really . . ."

He turned away to sift through some cuts of meat in a corner of the rank room.

"No," Anna said, "this will do fine, this one here."

Oh, do let me get out of here, she thought. *Hurry, hurry, hurry—I have to get home.*

But he was intent and finally flourished something that seemed bigger and redder than the bone he had previously found. Anna smiled and nodded and in every way tried to express gratified approval, but all the time her mind worked with dread.

What horror! To be discovered. Why had she not thought of that? It never occurred to her that the loss would be considered anything but an accident. After all, she had found it on the carpet. It might have lain there for weeks. How unfair. How outrageous!

But why had she done it? What had possessed her! She was a thief!

No, she was not. She tried to steady herself. She was not a thief. Mr. Parrish was right. They would suspect the maids.

She realized that he was holding the meat out to her, had been doing so, and was staring at her with concern.

"Ah, it looks fine," she managed, and held out her basket for him to drop it into.

"Now, let me figure this . . ." The butcher reached for a grubby pencil and began figuring her bill.

Anna had turned to leave, but, anxious not to call attention to herself by any more strange behavior, she willed herself to wait.

They could not accuse her. No one would think of her. She was safe. She just had to behave sensibly. Not sell it right off, but wait a while. . . .

The horror of her situation dawned on her. She realized she would have to return the stickpin the next time she went to Lynthorpe Hall. Drop it on the floor of the library and pretend she had just found it. Could she do that? Why not? But what if she were seen? Oh, the risk! Yes, but there had been a risk when she had taken it, even if it had not seemed so at the time.

And if she were caught? She could be deported—hanged! Oh, God, and then who would take care of Lydia?

Lydia—that is why I took it, for Lydia—and now I will end up hurting her by the taking of it.

She blinked away tears that threatened to overwhelm her and dug in her pocket for a handkerchief, which only reminded her of the moment she had taken the jewel. It was a pale face she lifted to the butcher when he finally turned to her.

"Here we are!" he said jovially.

Anna smiled shakily and signed her name without checking the tally.

"Do you know anyone at the Hall named Betsy?" he asked.

"Betsy?"

"Aye, that's the one they said took the piece. An upper chambermaid, they said."

"Betsy?"

"Aye, Betsy."

"Yes, I know Betsy. She stole . . . she took the . . . the jewel . . . ?"

"That's what they're saying."

Anna thought she would go mad. She smiled at him again, her foolish, frozen smile, and said, "Betsy. I would never have thought it of her. Well, good day, Mr. Parrish, and my best wishes to . . . your family."

She let herself out of the shop in an almost complete trance of horror. Betsy. Betsy! But Betsy did not do it! *She* had done it! It would be Betsy who would be deported or hanged.

Oh, what can I do!

It was in growing despair that Anna trudged the weary miles back to the cottage. Her mind was numbed with the word *Betsy*, and she conjured up the maid's plain, broad face. She was a young girl from the village, in the Hall as a kitchenmaid, but Mrs. Ives had liked the looks of her and moved her upstairs. And now, because of Anna, her young life was about to be destroyed.

Well, she could not let it happen, of course. She would have to return the stickpin and explain how she had happened to take it. She would tell them she had meant to return it to the butler but had not been able to find him. Oh, but she had told Betsy she had not found it. Betsy would remember that.

Well, she would just have to defy their inquiries and stick to her story. Whom should she go to? Mrs. Ives, of course. Explain to her. She would be worried about Betsy and glad to have her character restored. Yes, she would go immediately. Now, before anyone came to take Betsy away. Before she was taken by the constable to the gaol.

So ran Anna's thoughts as she entered the gate and walked through the garden to the cottage door. Inside she found Lydia napping by the fire, and Miss Bennet, her knitting folded on her lap, also dozing. But the burst of cool air and the closing of the door awakened her.

"Benny, I have to go to Mrs. Ives. I have just remembered something I left undone yesterday at the Hall. I must hurry. Would you mind hitching the cart for me?"

Miss Bennet looked aghast at the change in their routine, but before she could speak, Anna put her finger to her lips and pointed to Lydia and beckoned the woman to the kitchen where she grasped her hands in her own cold ones.

"Benny, it is extremely important that I go now. Please. I will explain later, I promise. I will not be long."

Miss Bennet looked at her in silence and then turned, picked up her rough cloak, and made her way outdoors.

Anna ran to her chamber, where she hefted down the box and dug among the shells, a pressed flower, a lace she had cut from one of her mother's gowns—she swallowed hard—and lifted out the handkerchief at the bottom. She opened it carefully and there was the stickpin.

As big as an egg, indeed!

She folded the pin back in the cloth and went swiftly down the stairs and outside, where poor, shivering Miss Bennet held the donkey by the reins, distastefully wiping her free hand on her skirt. She loathed performing this kind of chore and fought to hide her loathing from Anna, who always pretended she had not noticed. But today she truly did not notice and barely managed a curt nod before she got into the cart and urged the animal forward.

She was grateful for the chance to marshall her thoughts and plan her speeches. She must save both Betsy and herself. She would first talk with Mrs. Whitaker to find out exactly what was happening, then she would decide what to do. She would need a plan, some excuse. Perhaps she could pretend to have lost something herself and, in looking for it, "find" the jewel.

She bit her lip. She should have brought something from home, some pretext for visiting. Mme. d'Arblay's novel! No, Mrs. Ives had read it long ago, and besides, why would it not have waited until her next visit? She should have waited.

Oh! She would ask Mrs. Ives for her wages—she had forgotten about them. That would explain her immediate return—it would have to.

But what if they had already taken Betsy? What if she could not get access to the library? What if she were accused in Betsy's place and taken off this very day?

She had not explained anything to Miss Bennet or Lydia. They would not know where she was. What if she were deported? What if she were hanged?

All her *what if*s reduced her to quivering fear. A torrent of nerves swept over her, and she sat trembling and crying on the seat of her cart. She let the donkey come to a halt, dashed the tears from her cheeks, took a couple of deep breaths, and scolded herself sharply.

You will just go in there and tell Mrs. Whitaker that you found it yesterday and meant to return it, and the butcher reminded you that you had not. You had not even known they were real jewels. Just bits of glass you had not examined too closely, and you will brazen it out, and they will have to accept your word. Betsy will not contradict you, she will be too grateful. They may never allow you to come to the house again, but so be it. You will at least be safe, and so will Betsy.

With a last deep breath Anna kneaded some warmth back into her hands and picked up the reins to continue the long drive.

Just before her lay a rise in the road where the land swelled and overlooked the great wide valley of the Esk. Suddenly from over the rise came the same crashing of hooves and rumble of wheels that had overtaken her yesterday. Today she had not even the wit to urge the donkey to the side of the road, when all at once she looked up in horror to discover red horseflesh, flailing hooves, and the great high wheels of some awful apocalypse bearing down on her.

Chapter Five

ANNA KNEW SHE was dead. That was a certainty. She also knew that she would not have to worry about the stickpin. She lay quite still, waiting to learn just how heaven, which she was entirely sure was her destination, would welcome her. She waited for the voice of an angel or gatekeeper to call her name.

"I cannot believe it. You!"

She lay quite still, marveling at this approach.

"Are you dead?"

Of course she was dead—why else would she be in heaven?

Suddenly she felt a prod at her hip, and her eyes flew open in outrage.

"You are not dead."

Anna looked up into the scowling, wrathful face of Lord Crewe.

She sighed. "You are not an angel."

"Angel! Are you mad, woman! Yes, mad, that would explain it."

"I am alive," Anna said with some disappointment.

"Yes, you are alive. Not my choice, but that seems to be the case."

She sighed deeply. It had been nice to be oblivious for a moment; now she was aware of aches, confusion, and worst of all, her skirts lying somewhere in the region of her knees and a very cold wind on her legs.

She sat up instantly and was rewarded with a blinding pain in her head which called forth a moan, but still, as she put her hand up to feel the lump forming on her skull, she also managed to arrange her skirts to cover her legs.

"Is that not just like a woman! You may have a broken skull, but you will first see to your skirts!"

Anna regarded him through narrowed eyes. He loomed above her and was making no effort at all to come to her aid—and he was laughing!

"You are laughing," she said accusingly.

"Better than swearing, cursing, and giving you the trimming of your life which you so well deserve."

She drew her feet under her and made to get up so that she could carry on the conversation from a more dignified position. He did not offer her his hand, and she found that the pain in her head was worse when she moved, and she was suddenly so dizzy that she thought with absolute horror that she was going to be sick. She collapsed back upon the dirty roadway.

When she came to the second time, she was lying across Horace Crewe's lap, and he was cradling her in his arms, holding her head and shoulders. Something scratching at her cheek made her realize he had wrapped his enormous caped greatcoat around her. She quickly closed her eyes and thought furiously.

How was she going to get out of this? Between losing consciousness and lying in his lap, she would choose losing consciousness. She tried to faint again but could not; her mind remained steadfastly conscious. She struggled to release herself, and as she lifted her head, her lips came directly in contact with the softest lips she had ever imagined, lips that were pressed against hers in a miraculously gentle and welcome kiss.

Her eyes flew open and discovered the smoky eyes of a complete stranger who watched her as he kissed her. He lifted his head from hers and grinned. "I usually do not kiss unconscious women, but I really could not resist. You may be a pest on the public roadway, impossibly rude in the drawing room, but you are quite beautiful."

Anna looked at him dreamily as she relaxed back into his arms and studied his face. She felt a drowsy smile spread itself across her own and thought in a very distant corner of her mind that she was indeed mad. But mostly she focused on the fact that she was not in pain, lying here in this way, that she was very warm, that his arms were very strong, and would he kiss her again, would he, another kiss, would he kiss her . . .

He did. Those very soft lips came down on hers again, and she lifted her head to welcome them, then opened her lips and they came closer together in that kiss than she ever knew a man and a woman could come. She became vaguely aware that the lips began to withdraw from hers, to lift away, and she lifted her head after them, trying to keep that softness against her mouth. But abruptly they were gone, and her head dropped to his chest.

"Enough, girl! No more kisses for you. Let us see what this wound looks like."

Anna blushed and tried to wiggle away as his fingers gently explored her head under the cascade of loosened auburn hair. She gave a gasp of pain as he found the spot, and bit her lip as he parted her hair to look at it. He turned her face toward his and pried apart her eyelids which she had squeezed tight against the pain. He gazed consideringly into her eyes.

"I think you will do. It is a nasty lump, but I do not think it has addled your brains any. That is, any more than they were addled already."

She looked heavenward and tried to pull away, but her skirts were tangled, and she could not get free.

"Any more wounds? Maybe I should check. I do the vetting on my hounds, you know, so I am well qualified."

"Stop it! Do not dare touch me! Oooooooooooh!"

She had pulled away from him so sharply that it set her head throbbing. She tried to crawl while holding her head like a cracked egg in her hands.

Kneeling, she was at the same level as he, sitting on the grassy verge, where he watched her with traces of both concern and amusement on his face. She gingerly moved her head and saw the cart standing in the roadway; one of the wheels had snapped off and angled crazily from the body of the cart. The donkey was unhurt and enjoying an unexpected feast of tender shoots of grass. On the other side of the narrow track, the baron's curricle, looking smugly uninjured, and his magnificent horses, both of them gazing contemptuously about, were, Anna thought with relief, uninjured as well.

"Yes, all present and accounted for except for that cart of yours, which looks as though it probably should have been retired years ago, anyway."

Anna scowled. "It was retired—that is why we got it free." Then she bit her lip and suddenly exploded. "What have you done? Look! You have ruined my cart, broken my skull, frightened me out of a year's growth, and all because you have to drive that vainglorious, toplofty, pretentious rig and risk the lives of every decent person in Yorkshire."

"Every single one?" he asked with mock concern.

"I hate you!" Anna said and suddenly burst into tears. She could not stop the sobbing that broke from her.

"There, there," he said, and she felt a cloth on her cheeks mop up the wetness. She sniffed noisily and, pushing herself against him, managed to rise to her feet, although she staggered in doing so. But her head cleared, and although she was able to stand unassisted, she found that she was really quite shockingly dizzy.

The baron stood, too, and regarded her with mock suspense as she tried to maintain her upright posture and not collapse in an undignified heap at his feet. She tottered to the cart and leaned against it gratefully.

"Now what?" he asked.

She looked about her again, realizing that she had no way to get anywhere, that all she wanted was a bed and not to have to think about moving herself one more inch.

"Where were you going?"

"Lynthorpe Hall." No sooner had she said the words than she remembered her purpose for going there, and she staggered against the cart. Oh, no, she would have to go on, and she felt so terrible.

He had come nearer when she blanched. He inwardly cursed that he should be embroiled with this woman, but there was no question that she was injured, that he was responsible, and that he must not quit her until he had settled her with someone who could take care of her.

"I suggest you return to your home, as you are in no condition to pay visits."

"No, I must go on, it is quite important."

"Is your business with Mrs. Ives?"

"No. Yes."

"Some urgent sewing?"

"No, of course not."

"Some important novel to mangle with accents?"

"You are being rude."

"What is it, then?"

"Nothing that is any business of yours."

He could see that her knuckles clutching the cart rail were white.

"Listen to me. You should be in bed. Let me take you

home. Mrs. Ives will understand putting off your visit. I promise to drive back and tell her what has happened," he added magnanimously.

"No, she was not expecting me. It was something else."

"Well, all the better, then. I shall return you to your home and then take off back to London. In any event, it would probably not do to go there today. There has been some unpleasantness, and I am sure that they would prefer to be left undisturbed."

"Why? What has happened?"

"A maid stole one of my jewels."

"One of *your* jewels!"

"Why, yes," he said with raised eyebrows.

"What was it?"

"A mere trifle. A stickpin."

"What makes you think it was stolen? You may have only misplaced it!"

"I beg your pardon. I hardly think the thing concerns you."

But Anna knew it did, and knew further that this was the moment for her to do what she had to do. Maybe it was better this way. Maybe those at Lynthorpe Hall need not know. Perhaps she could continue to be employed there.

She steadied herself against the cart, turning slightly so that the sun was behind her and she would not have to look into its glare.

Taking a deep breath, she looked him in the eyes and said, "I have your stickpin."

Chapter
Six

THE BARON WAS startled. Whatever he had expected her to say, it was not that. "I beg your pardon?"

Anna felt weary. "I have your stickpin, with the emeralds and rubies."

"You have it? How did you come to have it?"

"I found it," she said steadily, looking into his eyes. "I found it yesterday, on the floor of the library, against the leg of the big table there."

"Found it?"

"Must I repeat everything?" she said, eager to be done with this horrible conversation. "I found it on the carpet. It must have slipped from your cravat and fallen to the carpet without your being aware."

"I see."

"Did it never occur to you that you might simply have lost it?"

"Of course it did, and the butler kindly organized the servants to look for it. A maid named Betsy searched the library, and a footman recalled her behaving quite suspiciously. One thing led to another, and it became clear that the girl had found it and decided to keep it."

"That would have to be Hawkins. You cannot trust him, he is a troublemaker. This just does not make any sense."

The baron shrugged. "It made sense to Ives. It need not do so to you."

"What has happened to Betsy?"

"Betsy?"

"The maid, you idiot."

"Idiot?"

"Oh, stop it. Betsy, the maid who is accused of stealing your stickpin. What has happened to her?"

"Nothing. She is being kept at the Hall until it is possible for her to be removed to the gaol at York."

"Well, she will have to be let go. I told you, I have it. I found it in the carpet in the library. I picked it up, intending to give it to Anderson, the butler, but I forgot. When I heard this morning at the butcher shop that Betsy was suspected, I realized that I still had it and must come to return it."

"Yes! I remember now. I encountered you coming from the library. You looked shocked. How deflating . . . I thought your shock was due to the impact of my charm and manly beauty. But instead you had just found my stickpin, although why that should have been shocking I fail to understand."

Lord Crewe raised his quizzing glass to study Anna. She struggled with the impulse either to kick him in the shins or to burst into tears, but her aching head held her hostage against any recklessness. She simply stared back at him in what she hoped was her most dampening manner.

"Where is the stickpin, then?"

"Such a trumpery piece of jewelry. Such foppery!"

"I believe that I need not suffer your insults. All I know is that you have property that belongs to me, valuable property at that."

"I daresay."

"You sneer at it, do you, Miss . . . Miss . . . Brown, was it not?"

"Smith."

"Ah, yes, Miss Smith. Where, I repeat, is it?"

"Here," she said, reaching into the pocket and withdrawing the crumpled handkerchief and handing it to him.

He took it with distaste and gingerly began to unfold it.

"Be careful! You will lose it!"

"I do not think so. I have no intention of losing it again, believe me."

Anna ignored the tone of his voice and turned away to study the horizon. *Oh, let this be over soon,* she thought.

"Yes, this is it." He folded it back into the handkerchief and began to study Anna measuringly. Several minutes passed while he studied her. She grew uncomfortable but staunchly returned his gaze, refusing to flinch or blush.

"Is this a staring match, then?" he asked.

She lowered her eyes momentarily but then looked back at him. "My lord, I am not feeling well. I have restored your stickpin to you. Could we call it quits so that I can return home?"

"Of course. How could I be so remiss? But you must excuse me. My mind does not work quite so rapidly as yours. May I, just for the sake of enlightenment, go over the facts again? You found yourself in the library yesterday, you said?"

"Yes, Betsy had asked me to search for the stickpin."

"You found it, but you did not tell anyone?"

"I . . . I forgot."

"I saw you in the library some time after I left you in Mrs. Ives' room. Did you stay with her all that time?"

"Please, you have your property restored to you. Must I answer these questions?"

"If you would be so good. You were with her, then, that entire time?"

"No."

"What did you do?"

"It is none of your business, my lord."

"Indulge me."

"No."

"Oh, please do. I find myself so hopelessly confused."

Anna knew he was toying with her, but also knew that he had the right of it, being the injured party. "I . . . I was looking for someone who could pay the wages due me. Mrs. Ives forgot that her maid, Alice, was gone and could not pay them. I thought perhaps Anderson might be able to. I was waiting for him—for someone—who could help me."

The baron stared at her blankly. "Pay you?"

"My wages," she said through clenched teeth. "I am Mrs. Ives' *paid* companion."

"I see. You needed the money, then."

"Of course, why else would . . ." Anna saw the trap and skirted around it. "I earn my bread, my lord. There is no shame in that."

"Surely not. So you searched for the stickpin and found it in the library."

"Yes." Anna felt chill, not only from faintness and the cool air. A large part of it was due to the hauteur of this man who, it seemed impossible to imagine now, had once kissed her so warmly. Twice.

"And put it in your pocket."

"I beg your pardon. No . . . Yes. Not then . . . later."

"Did you see anyone besides me?"

"Ah, yes."

"Who?"

"Well, I saw Betsy . . . and . . ."

"And forgot to tell her."

"Yes. I was in a hurry. I had to return before dark."

"Of course. Heaven help all those who might be so unfortunate as to happen upon you on the road in the dark."

Anna ignored that and raised her hand piteously to her head.

Crewe paused, looking weightily at her. "It is in your favor, of course, that you were returning of your own free will to restore it to me."

"Thank you, Lord Crewe," she said icily, then with a sigh, continued. "It was when I heard that Betsy would be arrested . . . I could not allow that."

"What a noble sentiment."

"No, not noble. Just decent."

"What is your real name, Miss Smith?"

"What is that?" Anna looked at him, startled. "What do you mean?"

"Your real name. And do not tell me it is Smith, for I shan't believe it."

"My name is Anna Smith. I am sorry if that disappoints you."

"Where do you come from?"

"What business is that of yours?"

"You are my business. You had my property in your possession—I am sorry, but I have the right to ask these questions."

"Well, I do not think you do, my lord. I think you are persecuting me for your own carelessness. First Betsy, now me. And in my case, I am in no condition to deal with your questions, whatever you think."

"Where did you come from, Miss . . . Smith?"

"I live near the village. We have been here five years."

"We?"

"My sister and my gov . . . my friend."

"And where did you live before that?"

"That is none of your business."

"Where?"

"The . . . West Indies."

"The West Indies. You knew Kingston well, then?"

"Yes. I knew him very well."

"Kingston is a place, not a person."

The check on Anna's emotions broke. "Lord Crewe, you have your property, there was no theft, so there can be no prosecution. What you are doing amounts to harassment. It is bullying. I have no way to get home. I am ill and weak and cannot even walk. I am dependent on you for your assistance, and you have the choice either to continue to stand here hectoring me or to act like a gentleman and take me home."

The baron was silent for a while before he spoke. "You are quite right, of course. My manners are wanting. But I find the rules of conduct governing one's dealings with a common thief whom one has just run down with one's carriage—and who, moreover, is a strikingly beautiful woman—quite impenetrable."

"I am not a thief," Anna said wearily, glad that he was now going to take her home.

"But you are beautiful?"

She flushed and moved away from the cart toward the curricle. She had taken only a few hobbling steps before the baron swept her up in his arms and carried her to the carriage, where he gently lifted her onto the seat. After retrieving the reins and soothing the horses, Crewe sprang up to the seat and leaned toward her gravely to tuck the blanket around her.

Anna was startled when the bays took off at a gallop, and, not braced for the burst of speed, she was thrown against Crewe. He responded by putting his arm around her, transferring the reins to his other hand and slowing the team to a trot.

Anna struggled to be free of him, but weakness held her pressed against him, and in his arms there was security against falling off the seat, if nothing else.

"To think I have kissed a thief today," Horace mused aloud.

"I am not a thief, and I am very sorry I kissed you."

"You were not sorry at the time," he said with a laugh. "And to think I am holding a thief in my arms right now," he added, giving her a little squeeze.

"Stop it! Let me go!" she cried, pulling away from him, but his arm continued to encircle her. Suddenly, aghast at herself, she burst into angry tears and felt such a furious anger at this cruel and careless man that she blazed at him, uncaring of herself or her safety.

"It is easy for you to speak of thieves, is it not? Have you ever had to worry where your next meal was coming from? Have you ever gone hungry a day in your life? Have you ever lost home, family, all that you loved and valued?"

She broke off only to come at him again. "It is easy for you to blame others—you misplace something and someone must suffer, someone must be blamed and made to pay. You leave in your careless wake every sort of upheaval and grief. Did you ever spare a thought to what would happen to Betsy?"

"You did steal it, then."

"No!"

"You did. You took it because you need money desperately."

"Very well, yes, yes! I did take it! I was going to sell it stone by stone in York to obtain better medical help for my sister than she has received here in this godforsaken place with the handful of pennies I have."

There was a terrible silence as Lord Crewe, his jaw set, stared fixedly over the tops of the horses' heads and as Anna stared defiantly, through her tears, at a far point in the road. She waited, not knowing which she dreaded more, to hear him tell her that he was returning to the Hall to turn her in, or to her family to have her arrested in her own home.

"You have not directed me to your home."

"At the end of this road there is a fork and you take the left turning."

For a long time neither spoke. Anna waited, holding herself from him to the extent that she could, but soon she failed of that exertion and slumped against his chest and felt the warmth and security of his arm while paradoxically feeling the terror of the decision he might make.

She jerked awake as he said, "I have made the turning. How far is it to your home?"

"About a mile more."

He said nothing, but held the horses to their sedate pace as they measured off the final mile.

Unable to face her family in the uncertainty of her fate, she found the strength to push herself away and to ask, "What are you going to do?"

"Do?"

"Do not do that! Do not always repeat what I say like that!"

"Like that?"

Anna laughed. The last thing she had thought to do this day, she had done. Actually laughed.

"That is much better," Crewe said, looking down at her from a startlingly close distance.

Anna looked away to regain her composure. "What are you going to do about me? Are you going to expose me?"

"I have been considering my course of action. I have my stickpin back, as you have so insistently pointed out. I can forget about it, and it can be our secret, just between the two of us."

Yes, Anna, thought desperately, *let it be that.*

"And I could drive back to Lynthorpe, announce that I have miraculously discovered my stickpin in the pocket of my pocketless driving cape, and tell them to free forthwith the unfortunate Betsy, and ride away a hero to chambermaids and paid companions everywhere.

"Or," he went on, "I could drive from your home into York, obtain the constable's aid in the matter, and have the satisfaction of watching someone who so carelessly uses the public roadways arrested, tried, and hanged."

Anna felt a rush of nausea. Horace Crewe read the painful impact of his riposte in her face and regretted it. Regretted it? Why did he care if he hurt her? Surely this was the most obnoxious situation he had found himself in, being wronged on all points and feeling alternately boorish and fascinated. He looked again at the beautiful woman at his side, and an idea began to take shape.

"There is my home, to the right. There." Anna pointed to the cottage that, sheltered by the dense trees, looked every bit as dark, damp, and uncomfortable as it in fact was. Still, it had never seemed so welcome as now.

"Please." She put her hand on his arm. "Tell me, my lord, please, do not torture me this way. Tell me, before we go in—what will you do?"

Crewe placed his hand over hers and turned to look into her pale face, into eyes huge and deep with fear, at lips tremulous and beseeching. He almost kissed her. Instead he smiled.

"So long as I find you beautiful, I shan't tell your little secret. It shall be between us."

"What does that mean?"

"It means, my dear Miss . . . Smith, that I shall have the undoubted pleasure of having you in my power."

"That . . . you cannot do that . . . that would be cruel," she said, gasping.

He looked down into her face and smiled. "But not without its pleasures."

Anna closed her eyes. "What about Betsy? Will you at least go and see to it that she is cleared? Tell them you found it? Or, if you must, you may tell them that I took it, but whatever you say, she must be cleared."

"I agree. I will take care of poor Betsy. Do not worry about that."

"Do you promise?"

"Yes."

"Honestly? Really promise?"

"Confound you, I said I promised!"

"Thank you, my lord. But as for me, you cannot promise that you will not accuse me?"

"Oh, no. I can promise you something. I promise that I will not say anything about your having stolen my stickpin—for the moment."

"For the moment. Is that all I can hope for?"

"You can hope for much more than that from me," he said, looking at her unsmilingly.

"What do you mean?"

"I think you comprehend my meaning. But here we are. Allow me to help you down."

Anna looked blankly at the cottage, forgetting that she had been eager to return to it. All she could think of were his words, and she felt them as a death grip on her freedom and her future.

Chapter
Seven

AS HE LIFTED his arms to help Anna from the carriage, Lord Crewe felt curiously flat. To have a woman of unparalleled beauty—unprotected, dependent on thieving for money—at his mercy for her very liberty—why, then, was he more discomfited than triumphant?

She suffered him to help her from the curricle but squirmed out of his grasp when he would have carried her to the cottage. She paused to get her breath, then straightened her cloak and tapped gently on the door to give Lydia and Miss Bennet a moment to collect themselves.

It was immediately apparent that they had watched their arrival from the window, for Miss Bennet was standing, and Lydia had slipped her feet over the edge of the sofa; they both stared at her with wide eyes and open mouths. When Horace Crewe ducked under the doorjamb and straightened to his full height and resplendence, both of them entered a state bordering on paralyzed awe. It might have been comical, Anna thought, if she had been less terrified of him.

"I . . . that is, we . . . had a mishap in the road."

Lydia struggled to her feet and made a faltering effort to reach Anna before she was intercepted by her older sister and gently laid back upon the pillows. "Now, Lydie, I am completely unharmed. No fretting! How are you?"

"I am fine." Lydia managed a wan smile. "If we are both fine, then why am I lying here like this, and why do you look like that?"

Anna laughed and bent over to kiss her, but as she did so, her hand flew to her head against the pain.

"Annie!" Lydia cried.

"My la— Anna, sit down, you must sit down. What has happened?" Miss Bennet guided Anna to the wide chair that she customarily occupied and dared to glance at the baron's shoes.

Crewe stood silently at the door taking in the tableau before him. He saw a girl as beautiful as her sister lying pathetically on a sofa, a study in fragility and suffering. He had noted her faltering movements as she had striven to rise, had seen the devotion that passed between the sisters, and the retainer's concern. But chiefly he had seen the poverty, the scarcity of the furnishings, the meanness of the fire, the bite of the cold.

Motionless in the doorway, transfixed by the scene, he watched as the older woman hovered over Anna, removing her bonnet, untying and pulling away her cloak and lifting her feet onto a low stool. He wanted to leave. He did not want to leave. For the first time in his life, Horace Crewe, Baron of Trent, did not know what he wanted.

"But what happened?" the girl asked.

Anna looked up at Miss Bennet and managed a smile. "It was just one of those freakish things . . ."

Lord Crewe found himself saying, "I am completely to blame. I did not see your sister's cart and ran her over.

Your cart is damaged, I am sorry to say—one of the wheels has been broken off. I will see to it that it is repaired and returned to you."

Anna found herself staring at him in astonishment.

"And the donkey?" Lydia asked shyly, unable to look at the splendid man who took up far too much space in the cramped little room.

"He is fine," Anna said. "I left him there."

"Perhaps we could ask Grubb's boy to go after him," Miss Bennet suggested, finding it impossible, as did Lydia, to look directly at their guest.

An awkward pause ensued. Anna, who found that she was almost comfortable so long as she did not have to move, gazed blankly from Lydia to Miss Bennet to Crewe, expecting someone to do something. She could not understand why no one spoke.

Miss Bennet cleared her throat.

Anna glanced at her and at the baron and discerned a twinkle in his eye. She collected herself, blushing slightly, and muttered in a low voice, "Lord Crewe, may I present Miss Maria Bennet and my sister, Miss Lydia Smith. Horace, Baron Crewe of Trent."

Whatever awkwardness had been created by Crewe's mere presence was magnified upon his introduction. Both Miss Bennet and Lydia were stunned into profound silence. Miss Bennet stared blankly at Anna.

"Perhaps some tea?" Anna suggested, amazed that she would in any way prolong his presence, but unwilling to directly ask him to leave.

Miss Bennet, skirting past him as though appalled at the possibility of infringing upon his person, scurried to the kitchen.

Why has he not gone? Anna wondered. She looked into the fire, whose flames accomplished so little in the gelid room, and hoped that if she stared hard enough at the flames, when she looked up he would be gone. Instead she heard his voice and, when she did look up, saw him bending over Lydia. In gentle tones that Anna had never before heard him employ, he asked what she had been reading.

"Horace."

"Horace. That is my name."

"Yes," said Lydia, blushing.

"Do you know, I do not like Horace."

"Your name?"

"No, that Horace." Crewe nodded at the book in Lydia's lap.

"I do not like him much, either," she confessed. "But Anna thinks he is a good influence on me."

"Ah." Crewe turned his head toward Anna and found a look of gentle love on her face. When he turned back to Lydia, he saw the look returned.

He reached for the book and randomly turned pages, giving himself a moment to assimilate the scene before him and its intriguing implications. He was in the presence of young women who had been raised in comfort and wealth—their accents, their education, the devoted retainer, all spoke of a social position immeasurably higher than that which they now occupied. He tried to remember what reason she had given for stealing the stickpin. For money to buy medicines, she had said. Not to regain a lost way of life, but to make her sister well.

He looked at the young girl and smiled. "If Horace is not your favorite writer, then who is?"

"Oh. Well. Perhaps Cowper . . . although I love Richardson and Scott and Mme. d'Arblay, too. But I know I should try harder to appreciate Horace. I do try."

The face she lifted to his was alive with earnestness and intensity. She was not answering from convention, but from a deep involvement with her books, an involvement she expected him to share because those around her did.

"I tried hard, too, when I was your age. I did not succeed, however, I am sorry to say. One of the great pleasures of getting older is not having to read anything you do not wish to read."

Lydia's face glowed, and she threw a laughing glance at Anna. "Did you hear that, Annie? I am being encouraged to dislike Horace!"

Anna listened to their conversation with dismay. She did not want to find him kind to Lydia; she did not want Lydia to find him pleasant. She wanted Lydia to distrust him as thoroughly as she did herself.

That wish no doubt accounted for her dampening tone of voice when she said, "I hope, Lydie, that you will not use that encouragement to stint on the translation Benny set for you."

"Oh, no, Anna," Lydia said, stung and bewildered. Her sister never spoke to her in such a way.

Anna was immediately filled with remorse. "Forgive me, Lydie. I meant . . ."

"Oh, do not bother to explain, Annie. I know you feel unwell. You look so tired."

The baron turned to look at Anna, who blushed and turned her head away.

At that moment Miss Bennet returned with a heavily laden tray and the baron rose to take it from her, setting it on the table before the fire. Miss Bennet flushed up, pleased at his gallantry.

Anna had a sudden consciousness of the disarray in her appearance and, bending at the waist and reaching behind her, gathered up her hair and twisted it into the semblance of a braid, unable to do more.

Crewe gazed upon the grace of her movements, the intimacy of her gestures, the lift of her body against the fabric of her gown.

Startled, he reached for the cup Miss Bennet held out to him.

The women made no attempt at conversation but slowly sipped their tea, savoring it, looking into their cups as though in wonder at the mere sight of it. Crewe nearly laughed at the due they gave it, but remembering the paucity of their comforts and the absence of any buns or cakes with their repast, wondered just how rare an undiluted cup of tea was. The solemnity and reverence with which they sipped it argued that it was rare indeed.

"Oh, but this is delicious, Benny!"

"Yes, it is almost like before . . ." exclaimed Lydia.

There was a frown, a quick glance, a guilty look at the baron, and a charge of anxiety before Miss Bennet and Anna simultaneously spoke, all of which piqued Crewe's curiosity.

After a rushed beginning, Anna's speech faltered to a halt. All she could think to talk about were subjects forbidden by one circumstance or another—her family's past, Lynthorpe Hall, the stickpin, her injuries, her resentment at Crewe's hold over her—indeed, there was such a catalogue that she shut her eyes against them.

Crewe saw all that and knew he must leave. Conversation had become nearly impossible to sustain. Anna was silent, Lydia was abashed, and Miss Bennet so avid with both curiosity and awe that she was silenced by the contending emotions.

"I must take my leave," he said. "Thank you for a cup of excellent tea. There are a number of things I must look to before starting back to London. I will ask them at the Hall to see to the repair of your cart and the care of your donkey."

"Poor thing," whispered Lydia. "We shall have to give him extra rations to console him."

The sharp way Miss Bennet turned to Lydia suggested to the baron that she had been about to expostulate on the impossibility of extra rations, but had caught herself. What a lot of terrible choices they must be forced to make, he thought, if they must choose between food for a donkey or food for themselves.

Crewe was astonished to discover a fervent wish that he could simply give the woman the damned stickpin, a trifle whose loss would not affect his life one whit but which could radically improve the quality of hers.

He rose to leave and again overawed the women, who watched him as though unused to other human beings. He drew his coat about him and fastened it, looking tactfully at the fire since none of them seemed capable of coping with a direct look.

Then quite suddenly Anna rose and crossed the short distance between them. Her face was ashen, and she laid a hand on his arm and lifted her eyes. "My lord, could we have a word together in private?"

"Of course," he said, and looked around. "Where?"

Anna looked confused. She reached for her cloak, as though to go outside with him, but Miss Bennet tugged it from her. "You must not go outside. You are much too weak. You should be in bed."

"Yes, you should," Crewe said emphatically. "Where is your bed?"

Lydia ingenuously answered, "Her bedchamber is at the top of the stairs."

"Very good."

Before any of them could know what he intended, Crewe lifted Anna into his arms and swept up the stairs to the cold of the hall above. He carried her into the chamber and kicked the door closed. Holding her an instant longer than necessary, he then gently lowered her onto the bed.

Anna stared up at him, bewitched.

"What did you wish to say? But you need not say it. I know. Do not worry, your secret is safe with me."

"For now," Anna whispered.

"No. Forever."

"Forever?"

"Yes."

"Is that a promise?"

"Yes."

"Really?"

"Yes, a promise."

"A promise. Honestly? One I can trust?"

"Yes, wench, a promise!"

They heard Miss Bennet's firm tread on the stairs.

"But why?" Anna asked.

"Let us leave it that you stole a stickpin from me, and I stole two kisses from you. I really think, when all is said and done, that I got the better part of the bargain."

When Miss Bennet burst into the room, Crewe was unexceptionally standing with his back to Anna drawing on his gloves. He bowed to the governess, clattered down the stairs, bowed to a blushing Lydia, and let himself out.

Anna looked at the empty doorway, silently suffering Miss Bennet's ministrations. She felt her aches and bruises, she felt the cold, but even more intensely she felt something more. Something akin to disappointment.

Chapter Eight

THE NEXT DAY Anna slept. The day after that she slept most of the time. But by the third day she could no longer sleep and the thoughts that crowded in on her were worse than the pains she had slept away. Lydia and Miss Bennet attributed her silence and subdued spirits to her physical condition and asked no questions. But Anna's mind teemed with them.

By the fourth day, feeling nearly herself again, she came to a decision. They must leave Yorkshire and go to Bath.

She had thought it all through before even hinting that she was contemplating such an upheaval in their lives. There must be no loopholes to allow anxious fears to become reasons not to leave. There was no doubt in Anna's mind that it was essential that they leave for Lydia's sake, as well as for her own.

While she and Miss Bennet baked, and Lydia read, propped in a chair dragged in from the other room, Anna repeated over and over to herself, *If it has come to the point where I would steal to obtain money, then it is time to inves-tigate more honorable if equally unpalatable methods.*

The only honorable if unpalatable way for them to stay together would be to throw themselves on the mercy of her grandmother, Clara, the Dowager Countess of Tretham.

That evening, as they sat with their cups of tea—once again the weak, pale brew they had become accustomed to—Anna ventured upon her plan.

"I have given a great deal of thought these last few days, while I have been forced to remain abed, to our situation, which has become increasingly worrisome. We have been given the shelter of this welcoming cottage, thanks to you, Benny, but we have very little else. We have less than three pounds to our name, and that we shall spend on food in no time, leaving nothing for doctors and medicines that would benefit Lydie."

Miss Bennet raised her head sharply and stared hard at Anna. They had agreed not to discuss these matters in Lydia's hearing, and furthermore, the subject was closed. Their situation allowed no flexibility; they were here and they would remain here.

Lydia, for her part, was both discomfited at having the burden of her ill health mentioned, and delighted to be included in what appeared to be a council of equals.

Anna continued. "Lydie would benefit from a more salu-brious climate, from doctors who have a wider experience with disease, from the healing waters of a spa such as Bath." She took a deep breath. "We also need a change.

"This cozy, delightful cottage has been a haven for us in our worst times, but I think we have recovered enough now to make plans for the future. Without this interlude, we would have suffered cruelly. Thanks to your generosity, Benny, we have been able to remain together even though we have had few resources. But now it is time for us to move on. I suggest we go to Bath and put ourselves in the hands of our grandmother."

After exclaiming in amazement and shock, Lydia and Miss Bennet fell upon Anna with protests.

"What can you be thinking of, Anna?"

"Our grandmother! But you said that Grandmother would never have us!"

"And that is right, she would not have us, but then, we also never asked her. We knew she bore us ill will and thus never tried. She is as rich as Croesus, however, and it is time we face the fact that we need her, that we are not able to continue as we are without her, and that she is our grandmother."

"That is not a respectful way to talk about her, Anna," said Miss Bennet.

"If she had shown me any reason to respect her, if she had comforted my father for my mother's death, if she had tried to help him in his grief, he might be alive today. And if she had ever helped us, helped Lydie . . . but she did not. Now she must. She shall."

"Are you suggesting that you just dash down to Bath and beg her to take you in?"

"Exactly, Benny. Or rather, Lydie will. I think it will be Lydie who will win her," Anna added with a fond smile at her sister.

"But I am sure I could not persuade anyone to do anything. And she would frighten me."

"Pshaw, Lydie. You might act frightened, but you have a vein of courage in you that you draw on in order to endure your suffering. I would like to see Grandmother try to intimidate you."

Lydia blushed, pleased at being thought courageous, but still alarmed.

"If I sell the pearls, they should fetch enough for coach fare to Bath and the expenses of the trip with enough to pay our debts here in the village, and if we are very lucky," she added with a smile, "a few new gowns. And if you let the cottage, Benny, it would give you an income while we are gone. In short, I propose that we go to Bath and camp on our grandmother's doorstep until she takes us in."

"But Lydie cannot . . ." began Miss Bennet.

"It will be very hard on Lydie. But it is equally hard on her to remain here. I do not propose that we leave immediately. With more money we can afford to visit a doctor in York and try to build up her strength before setting off."

"But . . . Burleigh." Miss Bennet said the name apprehensively.

Anna, though prepared for the name to be spoken, was unable to marshal the easy dismissals that had cleared away other objections. She paused to gather her thoughts.

Lydia had never before been privy to the secrets that lay behind the events that had torn her from her home five years earlier. She knew only that her cousin, Burleigh, figured in the tale. She sat very still, hoping that Anna would continue and she might finally be told what had happened.

"Lydie is sixteen, old enough to be told of the events that so drastically altered her life. This concerns her, Benny. It concerns all of us."

Miss Bennet pursed her lips—not entirely from disagreement or disapproval of Anna's decision, but as much from reverence for privilege and rank. She so thoroughly abhorred the circumstances that had led to Anna's and Lydia's being deprived of their home that she could scarcely countenance any discussion of them.

Anna persisted. Addressing Lydia, she told the story of their last years at Dragonsmere.

"Lydie, you were only six when Mother died—I do not know how aware you were of the changes that overtook Father. He became quite depressed and could not shake his grief. He . . . he turned to drink and fell in with a group of men who took advantage of his goodness. He gambled to be part of their group, and he wagered increasingly large amounts of money. But that in itself was not so terrible, for at first he did not gamble enough to threaten our security. But he grew deeply ashamed of his life and finally became divided against himself. It was as though he lived in separate worlds, that of his friends—if they can be called that—and our world.

"Unfortunately, without Mother our world became more and more painful to him, reminding him of his loss, reproaching him for gambling. The years passed, and finally gambling led him into debt, the kind of debt that threatened everything.

"Lydie, you must promise to forgive him. It is very hard, I know, but you must try to find it in your heart."

"But of course I . . ." Lydia expostulated.

"Just listen," Anna said, holding up her hand. "As you know, Father was a consultant to the Navy. He advised them on setting up the Sea Fencibles, the link of ships around the coast to warn of a French invasion.

"While he was deep in his cups one night, he told the plans to the whole company, bragging, letting everyone know that he was not what he seemed—an old, useless drunkard—but a responsible and trusted patriot. He could not have known, of course, that a certain Mr. Bevaqua, who was also present, was a spy for France. He encouraged Father to talk, and Papa, I suppose desperate to impress the company, revealed to him—in great detail, I am sorry to say—the plans of the Sea Fencibles. Burleigh, our cousin, was present and witnessed the whole sorry affair. Although unable to prevent this Bevaqua from leaving, he was able to hush it up. But Father, realizing later when sober what he had done . . . took . . . He saw no alternative than that he must . . . take his own life."

"He was a . . . no!" Lydia exclaimed in horror.

"Say the word, Lydie, say it, nothing is too horrible that it cannot be said."

"A traitor?" she said in a small voice.

"No." Anna dropped to her knees before Lydia and took her hands. "No, he was not a traitor. What a traitor does he does for profit and gain—he does deliberately. What our father did he did out of shame, his need to command respect. Burleigh said he was pathetic, but never evil. Burleigh said, too, that it was so long after the creation of the Sea Fencibles, and Father had been so long away from the Navy by then, that what he described was probably long out of date. It never brought harm to England. You must believe that."

Lydia looked at her sister with brimming eyes and nodded dutifully, like the child she still was in many ways. But, showing her courage, she lifted her head and said, "All the more reason for us to go to Bath. For if people think he was a traitor, we can tell them he was not."

"Oh, Lydie." Anna hugged her and burst into tears. Even Miss Bennet was forced to wipe away a tear. It was a moment before the emotion passed and Anna could resume.

"Dragonsmere and the title went to Burleigh, of course, as the nearest male relative. We would have come into a considerable fortune had Father's debts not wiped it out. After the funeral Burleigh explained that Papa had left so many debts that we would be hounded by creditors and that he himself had no money, either, since the income from the estate had to be invested back into it to repair what Father had neglected.

"He showed us the necessity to leave immediately, and to live quietly without attracting notice so that Father's creditors would not harass or prosecute us for his debts. In addition he allowed me to have a few of Mother's smaller pieces of jewelry, which was quite generous of him, since all the Tretham jewels are to be held for the earl's wife—Burleigh's wife—when he marries.

"He has protected us from creditors and settled an income on us, a munificent one, given the poverty of the estate, and has done his best to pay it over the years, although it would seem that at present his affairs are so straitened that he has to miss payments from time to time."

"Most of the time!" sniffed Miss Bennet. "He is three quarters behind in his payments to you."

"Yes. Poor Burleigh. He must have a great many claims on his pocket."

"And you having to sell the jewels to pension off the servants he dismissed, too."

"I could hardly refuse to do so. Some of them had been with the family for thirty years."

"I am trying to say that I do not think you need be as grateful to him as you insist."

"That has occurred to me as well. It is one of the reasons I think we must go to Bath. Whereas Burleigh cannot provide for us, Grandmother can."

"Why does she not like us?" Lydia asked.

"Because your grandmother is a very proud lady, from one of the oldest families in England, and she had planned for Father to marry royalty, perhaps even one of the princesses! But instead he inconvenienced her by marrying our mother, the daughter of the vicar of one of the livings they held. It must have been enough to cause her apoplexy!" Anna smiled.

"But although she could not cut Father out of the privileges and rights of the earldom, she did cut him out of her life. To her loss. He might still be alive if, after Mama's death, she had offered him comfort."

Miss Bennet's bitterness toward the Countess of Tretham found modest expression in a decided sniff.

"I shall write directly and tell Grandmother that we are coming and warn her to prepare to receive us in several months. June should be a fine time to travel, don't you think?"

Lydia's glowing eyes revealed that no matter how contentedly she might lie on her sofa reading and working on

Latin translations, a trip to the south of England held all the thrill of adventure that her books promised but never accomplished.

Miss Bennet broke the spell. "You have forgotten the creditors, Anna."

"No, Benny, I have given them thought as well. How can they take what we have not got? And if they threaten to arrest or deport me, Grandmother would pay them, rather than let further scandal touch her name."

Miss Bennet pondered Anna's reasoning. Suddenly she smiled, a lovely smile that stripped away the years of sacrifice. "It might be a good plan, Anna."

Anna laughed in relief, and Lydia clapped her hands. Excitement touched them all. Anna, most of all, was relieved to have the cautious Miss Bennet's endorsement.

But Miss Bennet grew thoughtful. "While it is true that it is a good plan, I must insist on one thing. We cannot go unless we have word that Lady Tretham will receive us. We cannot take the risk of arriving with no place to stay, with Lydie having just accomplished such an arduous trip."

"But if I ask her, she will never accede. If, however, she is confronted with us as an accomplished fact, she will have no alternative but to take us in."

"It is too great a risk."

"Yes." Anna sighed, acknowledging the rightness of it. "Well, perhaps the pearls shall fetch enough to enable us to take lodgings for a short time. Then even if Grandmother does not receive us, we should still be able to pass the summer months in Bath."

"Only the summer? Then I should probably not let the cottage until we know for sure."

"Oh, Benny, do you think we can do this?"

"Yes," she said in her decisive way. "We must. This has all been very well, but you are Lady Anna and Lady Lydia Farrant, daughters of a peer of the realm, and it is time for you to take your rightful places in the world."

* * *

As the coach made its progress down from the hills overlooking Bath, Anna, Lydia, and Miss Bennet could see the whole of the golden-stoned city lying before them. It was a storybook town, climbing up the hills from the valley, its magnificent buildings appearing to be sculpted from the land itself.

Lydia and Anna pressed their faces to the windows of the coach to discover every clue about their new residence. A more staid but scarcely less excited Miss Bennet sat between them, keeping her eye on her charges, on the landscape, but mostly on the ramshackle young women seated across from them in the public conveyance who were no better than they should be and who afforded her as much consternation as they did Anna and Lydia undisguised fascination.

The last week had been an education for both of them. Neither sister had ever been so much in the world, and although dirty, noisy, and tiring, the world was turning out to be a delightful and altogether agreeable place.

Lydia had endured the trip with far less discomfort than Anna had feared. They had been able to obtain the services in York of a Mr. Jones, whose regimen of medicines had strengthened her sufficiently to endure the rigors of the journey without, however, seeming to alleviate the under-lying causes. Taking the trip slowly, allowing for late after-noons and evenings spent resting at inns, had the effect of prolonging the trip not only for Lydia's comfort, but also, it turned out, for the increase of incident and diversion along the way. Lydia was buoyed and strengthened by the sheer joy she found in traveling. Anna hoped that her energy was based upon health and not febrile spirits that might dissipate and leave her weakened.

Altogether Anna had had few such worries. Her grand-mother had actually replied to her letter and invited them to stay with her for a week. Anna had been astonished at the invitation, grudging though it was. Although she had taken the sensible precaution of reserving rooms at an inn, she knew in her heart of hearts that once Lady Tretham had seen Lydia, she would keep her with her forever.

The coach pitched down steep streets into the center of the city, and it seemed to Anna that all Bath was built at crazy, dizzying angles to itself. She marveled at the sight of so many people toiling up the hills and wondered how the invalids who flocked to Bath managed them.

"Oh, Anna, look at that hat!"

"Where? Oh, indeed. Goodness! Five plumes!"

They giggled, and the women across from them giggled as well. One of them said in a broad, almost incomprehensible London accent that she had once had a bonnet with ten purple plumes.

Anna and Lydia were beginning to realize that many of these stories were Banbury tales, and they enjoyed them all the more for that, the precise reason Miss Bennet enjoyed them less.

Anna felt at one with the whole world. Nothing could depress her high spirits—they were free of cold and desolate Yorkshire, the isolation of the moors, the dependency at Lynthorpe Hall, and their neighbors. She felt regret at leaving Mrs. Ives. When she had gone to the Hall to make her farewells, and to see with her own eyes that Betsy remained firmly restored to the place of trust she had previously held, the elderly woman had been charming. Sorry to see her leave, declaring that her days would be lonely without her, she had overwhelmed Anna with generosity—giving her clothes, a few simple gold ornaments for Lydia, and a gift of twenty pounds, an unheard-of sum. Anna had wanted to refuse it, but her new understanding of the difficulties that lay ahead prevented her from doing so. She had accepted it, wiped away tears of gratitude, and almost smothered Mrs. Ives in a farewell hug.

She—and the vicar—were the only people Anna would miss from their five years in the North. She felt as though she were leaving the wilderness for life again.

The coach, sounding its sheet of tin, tearing a swath through the traffic in the streets, disrupting everything with its noise and importance, raced down Pulteney Street, turned sharply, and drew up before the Lord of the Dance, the inn they would be stopping at.

"We're here!" Lydia raised her arms above her head.

Anna laughed and bounded from the carriage the instant the steps were in place.

With more decorum Miss Bennet descended, and together they assisted Lydia's alighting. Immediately Miss Bennet hired a boy to take charge of their meager luggage—they had brought very little with them but books and mementos, because Anna had been determined to ask her grandmother for new clothes, declaring few of their present gowns fit to wear in this fashionable city.

They made themselves comfortable in well-appointed rooms. Anna had entertained fantasies of presenting themselves directly to her grandmother, but she had been dissuaded by Miss Bennet, who had argued for the need to rest after such a long trip, so as to arrive looking less like beggars than equals.

They gave themselves over to the luxury of rest, calling upon servants to take away their gowns to be brushed and pressed and to bring them hot water for the hip bath they took turns using before the fire. After a light meal, they took to their beds and slept the excited, contented dreams of arrival.

Chapter Nine

THE COUNTESS' FOOTMAN bade them wait in a small room off the hall while he went to inquire if Her Ladyship was receiving. Anna chaffed at the rudeness.

They had risen early to prepare themselves, lavishing their greatest care upon Lydia's appearance. The hack had driven them through broad and elegant streets, past rows of buildings with facades at once simple and festive with repeated patterns of columns, pilasters, and fan windows. Eventually they climbed a long hill alongside an open greensward where ahead of them shone brightly an unbroken crescent of brilliant white buildings stretching the entire width of the park.

At the center house, the keystone of the elegant curve that comprised the Royal Crescent, the carriage came to a halt, and Anna requested the footman's assistance in helping Lydia up the long stairs. The identical rudeness that required them to cool their heels awaiting their grandmother's appearance had manifested itself earlier when the footman approached Lydia as though she were no more than a common beggar on the streets.

Now they waited, Lydia on a red enameled chair, Anna at her side with defiance on her face. Miss Bennet, refusing to sit, struggled to appear as if she were not wishing she had not supported Anna's scheme.

Anna let her eyes feast on the marble, gilt, polished woods, crystal, and luxurious fabrics with which even this lowly chamber was bedecked, and realized that the magnificence did not intimidate her. A child raised at Dragonsmere could not be intimidated by this. But it was borne in upon her, as her gaze traveled along the domed ceiling down the portieres to the marble floor, how starved she was for comfort and beauty. What intimidated her was her own hunger, how very much she wanted this for herself again, and consequently how vulnerable she was to her grandmother's power to accept or reject them.

After a delay no doubt calculated to insult them, and with apparent surprise on his face, the green-liveried footman returned to announce that Her Ladyship awaited them in the gold room.

Anna, instructing the footman to give Lydia his arm, followed him with Miss Bennet up wide stairs whose walls were hung with portraits of ancestors whose features were familiar to her from portraits that had hung at Dragonsmere.

The footman halted before great double doors in a spacious hall lined with statues and mirrors. He knocked before throwing open the doors, and stepped forward to announce their names. Then he backed away, leaving a trio of women standing within its frame. One was a woman of twenty arrayed by nature in brilliant colors, with glowing health and sparkling eyes that took in everything. The second was a gaunt, older woman whose posture and lowered eyes proclaimed her a dependent but whose quietly assessing glance had missed nothing.

But to the two people at the other end of the long room,

it was the small young girl, pale and golden like a ray of light, holding her chin proudly and watching them with quiet, blue eyes, who transfixed them.

"Edward!" the woman cried out, lifting her hand to her throat.

The pudgy man at her side simply gaped.

"Grandmother," Lydia replied with a small curtsy.

Anna had not been prepared for the emotion that flowed between her grandmother and Lydia. The older woman, seated in a heavy, ornate chair to the side of a wide fireplace, stared at Lydia as though she were her own beloved, resurrected child.

Nor had she been prepared for Lydia's response.

Moving away from the support of the doorframe, Lydia walked slowly into the room, so slowly that Anna found herself holding her breath. Her back straight, her head high, Lydia displayed a poise that belied the isolation from society her illness had forced on her.

As she approached her grandmother, the two regarded each other without once looking away. They continued to gaze at each other after she came to a halt a few feet away.

The fat young man, who had recovered himself sufficiently to close his mouth, leaned down to whisper something to the older woman, but she waved him away, not taking her eyes from her granddaughter's face.

Finally Lady Tretham rose. She stood for a moment and then walked to her granddaughter, reached out, and drew her to her. The silence in the room as the two embraced was compelling. She stepped back, holding the girl's face in her hands, and shook her head.

"You are Lydia. Is it possible? You are the very image of your father when he was a boy. How beautiful you are."

Lydia was faint with fatigue and emotion and reached around her grandmother to lower herself into the chair her grandmother had vacated.

"Here, you must not sit there!" the heavy young man expostulated.

"Oh, forgive me," said Lydia, struggling to rise again.

"Nonsense, child. You sit right where you are." Turning toward the other women, who had remained near the door, the countess said, "And you must be Anna."

Anna went forth to be greeted. The embrace her grandmother bestowed upon her was perfunctory, and Anna closed her eyes, refusing to acknowledge the wish that it had been warmer. When they drew away from each other, her grandmother's eyes immediately sought out Lydia again, as though unable to get enough of the sight of her.

When addressed by Anna, she turned a distracted face. "This is our governess, madam, Miss Maria Bennet. My grandmother, Clara, Countess of Tretham, and my cousin Burleigh, the present earl."

As Miss Bennet curtsied, Anna approached her cousin. "Burleigh, it is good to see you again. We are so much in your debt. It is impossible for us ever to repay all your kindness to us."

Burleigh stood rigid, staring first at Anna, then Lydia. Finally, as though having resolved an internal dispute in her favor, he relaxed sufficiently to smile and come forward to kiss her on the cheek while managing a few awkward pats on her shoulder.

Servants were summoned to group the chairs so that Lady Tretham might sit close by her younger grandchild and to bring coffee which she announced she was providing for her guests even though it was a custom she not only did not partake of, but also thoroughly disapproved. An awkward silence ensued as they sat in a circle of gilt chairs facing one another.

Anna was dizzy with tremendous, almost overwhelming relief. They had arrived, they were in Bath, and their grandmother not only had accepted them, but was genuinely moved by her reunion with Lydia. What puzzled her was

Burleigh. He seemed to be laboring under the influence of strong emotion, and she could only hope that in view of her many creditors, he did not find their coming completely unwise.

"Well, well. So you have come to see your old grandmother at last."

Anna looked at her grandmother, incredulous. Miss Bennet cleared her throat to prompt her to a response. Struggling to ignore this outrageous interpretation of the estrangement, Anna managed, "Yes, Grandmother. Our meeting is long overdue."

"What were you about keeping yourselves in Yorkshire, for heaven's sake? I could understand it if you wanted to hunt, but you girls do not hunt, do you?" The countess looked at the sisters closely, as though only now taking in their appearance. "Heyday! Look at your gowns! Is this what passes for fashion in Yorkshire?"

Anna exchanged a glance with Miss Bennet. How was it that the countess had no understanding of their true circumstances? "We lived in Yorkshire, madam, because Miss Bennet has a cottage there and was kind enough to allow Lydie and me to live with her."

"Why would you want to live with her buried away up north? Why did you not come here or to London? I would have imagined young girls choosing a place with some life to it!"

"It was good of Benny to take us in, Grandmother. As for why we did not come here, to speak honestly, I did not think we would be welcome. And as for London or any other fashionable place, we could not have afforded it." Anna spoke all this looking straight into her grandmother's eyes. Her grandmother might have deluded herself about their condition in life up to this moment, but Anna would not permit her to continue.

"That is not what Burleigh told me. Burleigh said you had no interest in an old lady like me."

The countess was a tall woman whose back was as straight as her principles and whose head was held high, as though perpetually bearing upon it the jewels of her station. Her bearing was calculated to intimidate lesser mortals, and there was no doubt, Anna thought, that even the rich, stiff fabric of her gown was chosen to contribute to her unapproachability.

It was almost with hilarity, then, that Anna greeted her claim to be an old lady abandoned by her thoughtless granddaughter. She cocked her head and regarded her grandmother speculatively.

"Are you not going to answer me, girl?"

"I was considering the best reply, madam. Burleigh has protected our retreat from the world—perhaps he went too far in discouraging you from contacting us. But to be fair, it does not seem that you have suffered from our absence."

"No, why should I suffer? Well, I admit I did wonder about you from time to time. Now, what is this about my granddaughter Lydia being ill? You are pale, to be sure. What ails you?"

"No one knows, Grandmother," Lydia replied quietly. "I think that is what Anna wanted to come here for, to find a doctor who might discover the cause and know the cure."

"You have come to the right place. You could not find a better doctor than Gibson. I shall have him look in on you tomorrow." The countess bit the inside of her cheek and stared calculatingly at Anna.

Anna might have flinched from such a regard from anyone else, but she felt she owed her grandmother little. It was indifference that saved her from embarrassment.

"No money, you said. Why do you not have any money? Do you mean to tell me that that mother of yours spent every last farthing?"

"I do not wish to discuss this now, Grandmother."

"You do not wish? Well, I wish. Why have you no money?"

"Perhaps," Anna said, rising, "you will allow Lydie to be given a quiet room to rest in."

Anna stared at her grandmother, and her grandmother stared back in what they both knew was a challenge to the older woman's authority.

Burleigh, silent throughout the conversation so far, burst out, "Anna! That is no way to speak to your grandmother, who has been so generous as to agree to meet with you."

"I am not aware of having spoken in any way improperly, Burleigh. Lydie is ill and requires rest. Surely no one can gainsay that."

"Very well," the countess said decisively. "We will put you in the blue room," she said to Lydia. "Arrange it, Burleigh."

Burleigh turned red, staring at her and at Anna, but beneath the quelling gaze of the countess he summoned the servants and directed them to help the child from the room.

As the doors closed, she turned to Anna. "Have your trunks brought here. I can see that a week's visit will not be sufficient. That child is going to require a great deal of care. Let us say, the summer. Are you free to stay that long?"

Anna bit down her triumphant laugh. "Yes."

"Good. Then it is arranged. Now, you must excuse me, I am due at Lady Morris' this morning." The countess nodded abruptly at Anna, ignoring Burleigh and Miss Bennet, and swept from the room.

Anna was about to follow her out to join Lydia when Burleigh said, "Anna, a word with you."

"Of course, Cousin."

Anna turned back and appraised him. He was dressed in what she supposed to be the height of fashion, with a coat of peacock blue and breeches of a buff much too green for the coat. His shirtpoints and neckcloth were so elaborately exaggerated that they forced the folds of his heavy jowls to protrude above them.

But what especially drew Anna's gaze was the amount of jewelry upon his person. She recognized, with a clutch in the pit of her stomach, her father's heavy signet ring on his little finger and what she instantly guessed must have been her mother's emerald eardrops reworked into buttons on his waistcoat.

Anna stepped backward, stunned. For a moment she could only stare at him. She took in his thinning pale hair, his red jowls, and empurpled nose.

Finally she spoke. "You seem to be prospering, Burleigh."

"Yes, Cousin. My industry has been rewarded. Under my management the estates are flourishing, and I have been able to restore Dragonsmere to solvency."

"I am glad," Anna said quietly, truly glad for her home, forcing herself not to dwell on the fact that it was Burleigh and not herself or Lydia who received its fruits.

"But, Cousin," Burleigh spoke harshly, "you must know that it is madness for you to be in Bath. I cannot protect you here, you understand. And if your grandmother finds out the true state of your affairs, she will surely expel you."

"Burleigh, you must understand we may have been safe in Yorkshire, but Lydia has been declining year by year. What protection is it to live out of the world, away from creditors, away from gossip about my father's death, if only to lose Lydie in the end?"

"No, of course, she needs the best medical attention. You could find that at the sea, say, someplace like Weymouth or Cromer. But, Anna, your grandmother knows nothing of the dreadful state of affairs your father left behind. I have spared her, preventing her from learning the truth, and the truth about that other business as well."

"But what could my being here possibly do to change that?"

"The creditors, when they learn you are here, will revive all the gossip about your father's death. Too many people know the truth about that."

"Burleigh," Anna said, then paused, suddenly struck by her cousin's demeanor. He was perspiring, his forehead was beaded with sweat, and he had taken out a handkerchief, dabbing at his brow and wiping the palms of his hands. "Oh, Burleigh, you must not worry so about us. You are too good to us."

"Confound it, Anna! I am not saying this to be good . . . only to be good . . . but . . ." Emotion choked off his words.

"This is the way I understand it, Burleigh. Why should I fear the creditors? I have no money—they cannot take from me what I do not have. If they try to arrest me, frankly I shall simply turn to Grandmother and you. Neither of you would let Lydie and me be arrested or deported for Father's debts—if it should come to that. And if it should come out about Father, well, so be it. We will just stare the gossip down. After all, Papa is dead, and it is Lydie's life and health that we must consider now. Truly, Burleigh, there is nothing to fear."

The fat man stared at Anna in consternation, but she laid her hand on his sleeve and looked into his eyes. "Dear Burleigh, tell me I have not done wrong to come here, that everything will be all right."

Burleigh looked at her radiant smile, her lustrous eyes, and had an idea that startled him both for its simple right-ness and for never having thought it before. With greater address than he had exhibited heretofore, he bowed and smiled at her. "My dear cousin, you sweep all before you. You have won me over, and I am at your service."

He kissed her hand with a flourish, and despite her gratitude, it was all Anna could do to keep from pulling it from his damp clasp.

A few hours later Anna found herself rolling along in Burleigh's comfortable if conspicuous carriage. It was brightly new with green wheels and yellow upholstery and attended by coachmen decked out in scarlet and gold. From its high windows she looked out upon Bath with the eyes of one who now knew that she was soon to be part of its fashionable society. Her eyes glinted with green fire. She had arrived, Lydia would recover—she would never look back.

In the ensuing days Anna set a pace and style of living to which she intended to adhere for the rest of her life. She luxuriated. Her mind, cleared of the burdens poverty had imposed, focused only on the comforts at hand, and she relished them, wallowed in them, and took pleasure from them as she had never thought to be able to do in her life.

Her baths lasted until the water turned cold; her sleep, until she woke up satisfied; her time before the dressing table, until she found pleasure in her appearance; and she ate! She ate until she was full, she ate fruit until she thought she would grow vines out her ears, and she sampled cakes and pastries as they came from the ovens. Nothing in her life was hurried; nothing necessitous.

But one thing brought her even greater pleasure—spoiling Lydia.

Slowly a world began to take shape around her younger sister's needs and interests. She was ensconced in a lovely blue bedchamber, light and airy, whose windows overlooked the great park in front of the Crescent. The delicate moldings and graceful furniture made it a perfect setting for Lydia's fair beauty.

Within her reach soon accumulated an array of books that Anna brought first from the library and later purchased, with wanton disregard of the cost, in Milsom Street. Every novel about which she and Lydia had been remotely curious in the past, everything Mrs. Ives had especially recommended, Anna purchased for Lydia.

A mantua maker was summoned to the house, and long conferences were held over the styles and colors of new gowns for a girl of her age who had not yet had her coming out. "Anna, do you really think I should? I am only sixteen, surely too young to wear my hair up and these beautiful gowns," Lydia said doubtfully while fingering with great yearning the delicate muslins before her.

"Nonsense, Lydie, you will be attending social engagements with me and Grandmother when you are well enough. It is foolish to outfit you in little girls' clothes when you will soon shed them." Anna had another reason, not vouchsafed to Lydia, and that was, with so much pain and illness in her life, she could simply not now deny her sister anything. Miss Bennet's tight-lipped silences did not deter her, either.

She then set about interviewing nurses and soon found one whom they all liked. She was a west-country woman, Mrs. Brookens, whose good humor and robust ways were a delight. She took one look at Lydia as she lay on a gilt chaise with the sun streaming over her flaxen hair and lost her heart.

When Mr. Gibson, the physician, arrived, Mrs. Brookens mounted guard over her charge while he examined her, nodding emphatically when she agreed with him and shaking her head violently when she did not. Anna was delighted that her questions to the doctor and Lydia revealed intelligence and experience in dealing with the ill, as well as a great deal of common sense and a refinement of taste that would hold her natural exuberance in check.

Mr. Gibson sat a long time with Lydia, inquiring into her habits of sleep, exercise, and appetite. He watched her as she spoke, observing her gestures and strength, her facial expressions. He talked about her interests, watched her eyes glow when she spoke of Dragonsmere, where she had once had a small pony named Flurry, and of her books and of her sister, Anna.

When he examined her, he found much to concern him, but kept his counsel. Finally he was ushered into the salon, where Anna and her grandmother awaited him.

"Well, Gibson, what do you find in our girl?"

"Lady Tretham, Lady Anna." He sat and drew one booted foot over his knee and gazed at it reflectively. "I really cannot say. There is no apparent evidence of disease, which puzzles me, for there is no question that she is ill. Tell me about her." He turned to Anna.

"Well, surely you know . . . you have just talked to her yourself."

"Yes, but I would like you to tell me some things. Tell me about her mother's death, for example."

"Ah." Anna took a deep breath and looked askance at her grandmother, who had suddenly tensed.

"I believe Lydie took Mother's death very much to heart," she said quietly. "She was six. She had been a true hoyden, in love with life on her pony, terrorizing all the grooms with her daring. At that time she was not small as she is now. She was as tall as I had been at her age. I think it is her illness that has slowed her growth.

"When Mother died, Lydia retreated. She was there, but not there. And then when my father . . . my father was overcome with his own grief. He found it necessary to be often absent. . . . We . . . Miss Bennet and I tried to fill their places, but . . ."

Anna swallowed so that she would not weep.

The countess cleared her throat and spoke. "I am sure all this is very instructive to you, Mr. Gibson, but I cannot see what bearing it has on our poor Lydie's health."

"Well, Lady Tretham, she seems like a very unhappy child to me."

"Unhappy!" exclaimed Anna, tears filling her eyes.

"No, Lady Anna, I do not mean to reproach you. But there is an undeniable want of spirits."

"But that is because she is ill!"

The physician looked closely at Anna and smiled reassuringly. "This is just a hobbyhorse of mine," he said in a mollifying voice. "I think that the shock of her parents' deaths undermined her health. Whatever the cause, however, the cure will be the same in any case.

"I suggest that we proceed with the following regimen for the present." He outlined a course of exercise and treatments with the waters of Bath and other medicines he wrote down for them, and a diet which he copied out and gave to Anna.

Later, as she and Lydia sat quietly in the fading light of the evening, Anna reviewed the changes the doctor had recommended. Lydia wrinkled her nose at what seemed a great quantity of medicine and worried about an equally great amount of exercise, but Anna was able to reassure her that she would only do what she could as her strength grew.

"But what about you, Annie, what are you going to do while we are here? Not simply dose me and monitor my circumnavigations of my chamber."

"No, Lydie." Anna laughed. "I have my plans. As soon as you are settled into your routines, I shall begin to make my very pleasurable forays into the social world of Bath."

Chapter Ten

ANNA AWOKE AND stretched, enjoying the delicious feel of fine linen against her legs, the generous expanse of the bed—so wide that she could barely reach both sides—and the sure knowledge that she did not have to move until she chose to, and that she did not have to bake a single loaf of bread, peel a single turnip, or create a single fire from sodden lumps of coal.

Rolling over like a lazy, sun-warmed cat, she finally emerged from the covers and ran to the window to throw open the curtains without waiting for the maid. The day she beheld was golden and warm, and she turned with delight to the room where the gold-papered walls and thick golden patterned rugs caught and held the sun's brilliance. If the room had been designed for her, it could not have set off her beauty to any greater degree.

Stretching her arms over her head, she yawned and pirouetted with happiness. Quickly she wrapped herself in her old, soon-to-be-discarded robe, knocked on the adjoining

door, and slipped into Lydia's chamber, where the nurse
was already bustling about, and Lydia, sleep-tousled and
warm, greeted her gladly.

"Annie, this is your day!"

"Ah, Lydie, I shall make a fool of myself, I am so
excited."

"To spend the entire day at the shops—what bliss! Won't
it be wonderful to have all new gowns! Will you choose
muslins? Mull? Nainsook? Cambric?—Figured? Spotted?
Striped? Plain? . . ."

"Stop! You are all at sea. No muslins for me, said she.
Hmmm. How can I keep up this rhyme?—Taffetas, satins
alone will do, so says Lady Anna Farrant to you!"

"Oh, Annie, wouldn't it be wonderful if it were proper
for you to wear such fabrics?"

Anna shot her an amused glance but held her tongue.
"Well, dear, I must be going. I do wish you could come
with me."

Lydia, drinking an amber-colored liquid that Nurse
Brookens had poured out, wrinkled her nose and made
a sour face.

Anna laughed. "You look like a monkey."

"You would, too, if you were required to drink this awful
poison!"

Anna leaned over and dropped a sloppy kiss on her sister's cheek, looking at her happy face and sparkling eyes,
and wondered how on earth the doctor could think she was
unhappy.

"I have no idea when I will return, but perhaps we can
arrange to take you out in your Bath chair this afternoon.
You must employ all your arts to charm Mrs. Brookens into
letting you go."

They both turned expectantly to the nurse, who merely
smiled and said that she would judge her patient's condition
when the time came. Anna hugged Lydia and took herself
back to her chamber.

After a hasty breakfast, she left the house with Miss Bennet before Lady Tretham had made her appearance downstairs. Her grandmother made a habit of taking her breakfast in bed and routinely answered correspondence, consulted with the housekeeper, and accomplished many of her daily duties before descending by midmorning. It was an indulgence to her age, she had told Anna, and Anna welcomed the habit since she most certainly did not want her company on the shopping expedition. Miss Bennet's would be onerous enough.

They arrived at Mme. Fouchon's, reputedly the most fashionable modiste outside of London, and Anna explained that she was in need of nearly everything. Madame regarded her with a displeasure slightly leavened by curiosity. The young woman's garments were puzzling; the quality of the fabric was excellent, but the fashions were hopelessly out of date. She was about to dismiss her from her shop when Anna blithely added, "My grandmother, the Countess of Tretham, doubted that you would have the resources to undertake the fashioning of so many gowns, but . . ."

It was a treat to watch the modiste's expression work its way from scorn through blank amazement to the most ingratiating servility. Anna enjoyed it but thought with some bitterness that the change she had wrought had nothing to do with herself or her own qualities, but simply with the fact of her grandmother's wealth.

Miss Bennet chose a corner chair whence she could watch and prepared to enjoy herself, not expecting that Anna would need her since her taste was exceptional and she likely would be purchasing only a few modest muslin gowns, a cloak, and a tippet or two.

She was wrong. Anna soon had Miss Bennet and Mme. Fouchon on their heads. The two women, one outraged and not afraid to show it, the other outraged but fearful of offending a valuable customer, agreed only that all of Anna's choices were completely impossible.

Anna had carefully thought it all out. With her hair, fabrics in pinks and purples and reds would be the most dramatic. Not for her the boring pastel blues and greens that were the usual lot in life for those with red hair. No muslins, either. She had meant it when she had told Lydia that she intended to purchase only the richest fabrics. Of course, it being summer, she would agree to a few sarcenets and cambrics, but she returned bolt after bolt of suitable fabrics and continued to press for the more sophisticated ones.

The first gown she sketched out to the shopkeeper was one she had particularly admired on a guest at her grandmother's home a few evenings before. The very low neckline was offset by high puffy sleeves, and the skirts were slashed to reveal panels of a second color. She had dreamed of this gown for days, deciding to have it made in a soft shade of rose with a brilliant coquelicot for the panels.

It was then that Miss Bennet and Mme. Fouchon became agitated. "But it is impossible, my dear. Perhaps you do not understand, but the fashions here in Bath, for a young woman of your age, so young, so fresh, so unmarried . . ."

Miss Bennet was more direct. "Anna, you would not be allowed to leave the house wearing a shameless gown like that."

Anna did not heed them. She simply smiled a maddening, confident smile and asked to see satins in shades of violet. These she fancied made into a ballgown with a shimmering gossamer overdress of startling capucine that would look like the changing colors of a kaleidoscope.

Miss Bennet, by this time, was leaning against the counter fanning herself. Mme. Fouchon was ceaselessly rushing into the back room to calm her agitated heart and smooth her hair yet again. She could not allow these purchases. If she did, the countess would never pay for them, and she would lose the value of the expensive fabric. But, on the other hand, if she were to refuse the granddaughter of the Countess of Tretham . . .

Anna was unstoppable. There followed a deep indigo morning gown, a rich plum riding habit, a spencer and turban of naccarat and mulberry, a morone taffeta ballgown with a bodice that was to come to here—and both older women paled when Anna made the mark on her bosom that denoted "here."

Finally, seventeen gowns later, Anna turned her attention to the cloaks, spencers, muffs, pelisses, cloaks, and tippets she would require to wear with the gowns. All were to be lavishly trimmed with furs, laces, ribbons, and beads.

Miss Bennet finally relaxed. It had become so very outrageously expensive that Mme. Fouchon would never take scissors to fabric without the countess' explicit approval, which she was very sure Lady Tretham would never give. She hinted as much to the modiste, and together they ceased remonstrating, willing to leave the naysaying to the countess.

Anna finally was finished and ready to move on to other shops to select bonnets, slippers, perfumes, and perhaps a jewel or two.

Before she took her leave, she smiled at Mme. Fouchon and said, "Now, I realize that you are concerned about whether these styles are proper for a woman of my age. Please be assured that I have obtained my grandmother's approval for everything I have chosen—we had the most delightful time planning them. She was always such an original, my grandmother. And I am quite certain that she would be very annoyed to be troubled by yet another discussion of my gowns. Poor lady, I have taken so much of her time that none of us would want to take any more of it, would we? Of course not. Now, are there any questions?"

She smiled charmingly, her head tilted to one side. Miss Bennet and the modiste simply stared. The governess felt as though she did not know this young woman at all. Her Anna and these disgraceful garments? Had she and her grandmother connived at these designs? Miss Bennet found herself looking at the modiste, who was looking inquiringly at her. She drew herself up and nodded curtly. She would not display further uncertainty. If Anna said so, the dressmaker must oblige her.

After seven reticules, ten pairs of slippers, one pair of riding boots, twenty bonnets, and a variety of ribbons and plumes and lace had been purchased and after scents had been sampled and approved, and after the purchase of a number of rather simple necklaces worked in garnet, amethyst, coral, and amber, Anna declared herself finished.

Miss Bennet, who had acted the role of Greek chorus, running after Anna warning of the horrors of overspending, of angering the countess, of appearing to be a wanton and a spendthrift, of appearing encroaching and mercenary, had been—the fate of most Greek choruses—summarily ignored.

Anna stepped out into the sunshine of Bath Street and clapped her hands. "One more thing."

"What is that?" Miss Bennet asked wearily.

"A puppy for Lydie."

"A puppy? Oh, my, never, you never can, my lady. Her Ladyship would never allow it."

"Where does one find a puppy in a town, Benny? One does not go simply to the nearest farm and ask. Or does one?"

"We would have to inquire. Why don't we return and ask Craig for his advice?" Miss Bennet was well pleased with herself, sure of the butler's dampening advice.

But Anna returned to the jeweler's and asked the pleasant man behind the counter where they might find a puppy to purchase. The jeweler directed her to the confectioner's down the street who, he thought, had a young pug that had whelped not so long ago.

The confectioner's assistant's dog had had puppies but they were all gone; however, she knew where there was an old man who helped out at the haberdasher's who had a spaniel that had recently had puppies.

Miss Bennet insisted that they return home, that it was very late, that her course of action was unwise—but Anna sailed on.

At the haberdashery, in a box in a back room, they found a nest of lively pups and three kittens, and when they left the shop, Anna carried the sweetest little puppy. Miss Bennet held, against her will and with thorough disdain, a nondescript tabby kitten.

When they arrived back at the Crescent, Anna swept up the stairs with Miss Bennet in her wake and strode into Lydia's room, where she deposited her trophy on Lydia's lap. Miss Bennet grudgingly did the same. Then they stood back and saw Lydia, her mouth open, stare first at the animals, then at Anna and Miss Bennet, and back at the pets. Huge tears formed in her eyes, and her smile changed to a tremulous "Oh." They saw her hands move slowly to touch her new pets and then to scoop them up and hold them both against her cheeks. A look of such blind radiant gratitude shone on her face that Miss Bennet regretted her disapproval, and Anna was not even aware of her triumph. She was too busy wiping away her own tears.

Anna's siege of Bath's shops continued as it had begun. The next day she purchased a colt for Lydia, which she had arranged to stable within a block of the Crescent and which she had Lydia driven over to see from the carriage window. The next day she arranged for a jeweler to come, and she purchased a locket on a gold chain, simple pearl eardrops, and two delicate filigree bracelets for her sister.

Miss Bennet, protesting uselessly in what had become even to herself a boring monologue, could not prevail upon Anna to cease her mad spending. On the day the modiste's parcels arrived, Anna spent the morning trying on gown after gown after gown, running into Lydia's room, displaying them, and interrupting Lydia's morning studies and the regimen of rest and exercise. The only person she did not interrupt was her grandmother, who had gone out and would not return until Anna and Lydia had left for the Pump Room.

Finally Nurse Brookens was driven to shut and lock the adjoining door, and Anna, resplendent in an apricot-and-amaranthus walking dress with ruching on the sleeves and deep Russian-flame quilling banding the skirt, pirouetted before the mirror and looked with satisfaction at what she beheld.

She was especially pleased with her hair. During the years in Yorkshire she had worn it simply, uncut and uncurled, pulled back out of her way, outlining with a widow's peak her heart-shaped face.

When the countess' hairdresser came to the Crescent, she had eyed Anna while she worked first on the younger girl. Lydia's hair was simple to work with. They all agreed, although Lydia herself expressed some anxiety, that she should have her thick curly hair cut close to her head so that her face would be framed with golden curls. When the hairdresser finished, she stood back, her brush raised over Lydia's head like a conductor's baton, and seemed to orchestrate the happy exclamations that burst forth. It was a great success.

She had then turned to Anna. They eyed each other through the looking glass as though combatants. And indeed they were. It took all her perseverance, but Anna succeeded, and when the hairdresser had completed the scant trimming, which was all she had been allowed, she turned away muttering about dowdy styles and the mockery of the *ton*. But Anna was satisfied. She knew that the demureness of her hairstyle would form an interesting contrast to the boldness of her gowns.

As she watched Lydia being carried into the Pump Room later in the day, Anna did have a moment's doubt. Why did she wish to be so conspicuous? Why was she, so sober and sedate previously, suddenly demanding to be noticed and commented upon? She dismissed the question from her mind. She had access to money and she would enjoy what it brought. She smoothed the fabric of her gown, drawing pleasure from its sensuous feel, and moved through the throng next to Lydia's chair, aware of the looks that came their way.

The Pump Room was as crowded as Anna had been told it would be. She had not yet visited it, having saved her forays into the pleasures of Bath society for the moment when she would be suitably attired and Lydia strong enough to join her. She could recognize no one, for despite a few evening parties to which her grandmother had invited some of her oldest friends, she had met very few people. Burleigh, who had been at Dragonsmere since the day after her arrival, would have made a welcome escort.

She followed the milling throng in the perambulation of the room, glancing at people's clothes and bonnets, exchanging whispered remarks with Lydia and Miss Bennet, enjoying her sister's shining eyes.

At last they came to the stone fountain that held the famous waters. Anna obtained water for the three of them and they carried their glasses into a corner of the room away from the traffic and tried to drink it. The water, rich with minerals, rich with smells, was almost undrinkable, but Anna and Miss Bennet drank theirs down in companionship with Lydia, who was taking considerably longer.

Anna had just laid down her glass and was sympathizing with Lydia, trying to achieve another swallow, when suddenly she saw over her sister's head a figure that made her blanch.

It was Lord Crewe!

To Anna, one of the most forceful reasons for moving to Bath was to avoid encountering the man ever again. Despite

his assurances that he would never betray the secret of
her thieving, she did not trust him. The miles she had
driven away from Yorkshire were miles of safety between
her and that shameful act and the one human being who
knew of it.

Now here he was in Bath! If she had thought him anywhere but Yorkshire, it was London—Paris—one of the
fashionable places he had mentioned visiting this summer.

Oh, heavens! Anna turned away, bent her head, and
played with the folds of her skirt.

Crewe was approaching them in the circular orbit the
crowd took around the room. In a few moments he would
be past, and she could then persuade Lydia and Miss Bennet
to leave, even without Lydia's second glass of the waters.

"Oh! Look, Annie! Look, it's that man—the baron. You
know, the one called Horace. Oh! Hello!"

Anna was in agony to hear Lydia's excited voice and
ventured a glance that showed her Lydia's flushed face,
her hand upraised in greeting, and Crewe, about ten feet
distant, giving Lydia a most quelling glance.

Lydia was crestfallen. "Oh, he must not have recognized
me."

Anna turned her head away, irrationally furious with him
for slighting Lydia.

But she had not been quick enough.

Suddenly she heard him say from not more than a foot
away, "Surely it cannot be . . . Is it . . . Miss Brown?"

Anna reluctantly lifted her face, and he drew in his breath
at the sight of her. He beheld her face, her hair, his eyes
swept down her figure and took in her gown, her jewels.
Backing away he said, "No, surely this is not Miss Brown."

"No, it is not."

He approached, looking intently at her. "Ah! Miss *Smith*!
I remember."

"No."

"*Not* Miss Smith? Miss . . . Black?"

Anna looked to Lydia and Miss Bennet for help, but they were staring at Lord Crewe in dumbstruck admiration.

Anna cleared her throat. "Why, Lord Crewe, how pleasant it is to see you again. I had not thought to see you in such a place as Bath, not at an out-of-the-way watering hole like this."

The baron smiled. "I am equally surprised to see you here, Miss . . . White?"

"My lord, my name is not Smith . . . nor any of those others, or," she added, unable to resist, "Green, Blue, Red, or Puce, either."

"No," he said in mock dismay, "not Miss Puce?"

"No," she answered, trying not to giggle. "It is Anna Farrant."

"Miss Farrant."

"Actually it is Lady Anna," she added with satisfaction.

Chapter Eleven

"LADY ANNA FARRANT."

"Yes." Anna inclined her head, a smile playing on her lips.

"Would you know ... surely not." Crewe nodded as though to reassure himself of something and then favored her with a patronizing and supercilious smile. "How do you come by your title, my lady?"

"By birth," Anna said, trying not to let her enjoyment show.

"Ah, yes. I meant ..." The baron sought reassurance in his quizzing glass, which, with great concentration, he drew from its pocket and polished against his sleeve. "What I meant," he said again, bowing, "would you be related to the Earl of Tretham, of Dragonsmere?"

"Yes."

"I see."

Anna had to laugh. His frustration at being unable to place her surely, so as to know with what exact degree of respect to treat her, his unwillingness to ask directly what he wished to know, all combined with his unfazable hauteur, finally proved too much.

"Really, my lord . . ." She laughed, wanting to say how ridiculous he seemed, but controlled her tongue just in time. "Do you remember my sister, Lady Lydia, and our good friend, Miss Maria Bennet?"

The baron tore his wrathful gaze from Anna and bowed to the others. As he did, his gaze fell on Lydia, and he realized that the frail, delicate girl he had met in the cold cramped cottage was on her way to acquiring the bloom of health and beauty.

"Lady Lydia." He reached for her hand. "How well you are looking and how very beautiful!"

Lydia blushed and lowered her eyes, trying to withdraw her hand before the baron could brush it with the lips he bent toward it.

He accomplished the kiss and lifted his eyes, regarding her with such pleasure and warmth that Anna could not maintain her contempt.

"My sister is here for the waters," she said. "But as you can see, she is a reluctant consumer."

"She is certainly the finest recommendation for the waters I have yet seen."

Lydia, still blushing, exclaimed, "They are horrible! Why is it that all medicines are repulsive? You should be required to taste the concoctions that Nurse makes me drink. And although she has been bringing me this water to drink for weeks now, I still cannot accustom myself to it. No one ever warned me how horrid it is!"

"It is a conspiracy. If everyone admitted how awful the water is, no one could be persuaded to come here to drink it."

"But it is quite good for you," Miss Bennet said, anxious that Lydia not be talked out of drinking it.

The baron answered her with a bow and in a gentle voice

said, "Indeed, Miss Bennet is right, Lydia. You must not give up on such a proven restorative."

"I will not. You know," she added shyly, looking up at him through her lashes, "Annie bought me a puppy and a kitten. The puppy's name is Pamela, and the kitten's name is Clarissa. I have a colt, too, but I have not yet ridden it. Annie has had it stabled in the next street, though, and I have been twice to see it."

The baron glanced at Anna whose face was alight with pleasure in her sister's joy. Again he was moved by their bond. "You are lucky in your sister."

"Oh, yes," Lydia said and turned and clasped Anna's hand. "Yes, she is the most wonderful sister."

"Miss Bennet, will you please tell Lydie to silence her tongue and not to make these paltry attempts at flattery, because I will not be talked into buying her a goat, a camel, and three elephants to round out her menagerie."

Lydia and the baron laughed, and Miss Bennet smiled indulgently at her precious Anna.

Anna was amused at the baron having to confront her new guise as a titled lady, a change from desperate thief, to be sure. She lifted her face to his gaze and discovered him watching her with a cocked eyebrow.

"Is something amusing you, Lady Anna?"

"No, I was only smiling at the pleasure of being in the famous Pump Room."

"Perhaps you would like to take a turn around the room with me."

Anna would not have considered it for a moment except that Lydia said, "Oh, yes, do, Annie, and bring me a glass of water. I have to drink another before I leave, and it will take me forever."

Maneuvered thus, Anna could do nothing but rise and join the baron. As she glanced up into his face, Anna became aware, with a surge of warmth, that he had kissed her, had borne her to her bedchamber, and probably knew her more intimately than any man on earth.

She also appreciated the figure he cut. He was a very handsome man. There were few people by whom Anna could be dwarfed, given her stature, but the baron was one of them. Her head barely came to the top of his shoulder, and she felt light and dainty by his side.

"So, Lady Anna Farrant," the baron began, "the Farrants are very well known to me, but I do not remember an Anna . . ."

"Hmmm."

"You are not going to help me, are you?"

"No."

"Did you just discover that you are a Farrant? That must be it! They discovered you and bestowed the family fortune on you. I know, you were an orphan, left on the doorstep of Miss Bennet, and since I last saw you, an emissary from the family arrived at the cottage with proof of your identity, and yes! slipped a glass shoe upon your foot—the famous Farrant slipper—and . . ."

"Oh, stop being absurd," Anna said, laughing despite herself.

"If you do not choose to explain it to me, I am, forced to explain this metamorphosis myself. Let me think—I know!" He beamed at her and whispered in her ear. "You stole something truly valuable this time, valuable enough to afford this exquisite, if slightly unusual, rig-out, and to come to Bath pretending to be a Farrant . . ."

"My lord, you promised that was to be forgotten," Anna protested, trying to withdraw her hand.

"No, you don't," he said, clasping it firmly in the crook of his elbow. "I promised not to say anything about it to anyone else! But between us . . ." he added, with a lascivious wink.

"Are you never serious? You must promise me, now that I am in Bath and beginning my life again, not to . . . oh, it is so shameful . . . a stickpin! A foolish trumpery stickpin!"

"What is so shameful? That you stole or that you stole something so 'trumpery'? I admit—a fine moral point."

Anna looked away.

"Well, Lady Anna, your secret is safe with me, rest assured, but I do plead to know about your Farrant connection. It will be your payment to me for my silence. Farrants are my hobby, you see, one of my favorite people is one."

Anna looked up to see if he meant her.

"Vanity, vanity!" he said, laughing.

Anna allowed herself to nudge him with her elbow.

"And now violence upon my person. Help. Help!"

"Stop that!" Anna said through gritted teeth.

"Tell me, then. Just what kind of a Farrant are you? Are you any more familiar with the name 'Tretham' than you were with 'Kingston,' for example?"

"Of course."

"Would you know Clara, Countess of Tretham?"

"Yes. She is our grandmother—we are staying with her."

Lord Crewe stopped dead in his tracks, pulled away from Anna, pulled his quizzing glass from his pocket, and studied her with elaborate care. "Your grandmother," he repeated.

"Oh, stop making a cake of yourself and do put away that silly glass," Anna said, reclaiming his arm, and forcing him, with a small push, to move on.

"But you underestimate the depth of my amazement, Lady Anna."

"Humph."

"I have never heard her mention two such beautiful granddaughters. Nor two ugly granddaughters."

"I am not surprised," Anna said bitterly.

The baron was silent. "Ah. Edward's family."

Anna hesitated an equally long time before she answered. "Yes."

"And after his death . . . you moved from Dragonsmere to the cottage where I found you?"

"Yes."

"And now, a happy reunion?"

Anna was silent.

"What a lot is not being said here," the baron said seriously. "The countess is an austere woman."

Anna looked around the room at the people circulating in their finery, noting the headdresses, the gowns, watching the faces, the laughter, guessing at the confidences being exchanged between friends.

The baron followed her gaze. "You do not wish to speak of it further."

"Perhaps you can tell me something about the people in the room. Do you know any of them? Besides Lydie and Benny, I know no one at all."

Crewe complied, knowing full well that this was to divert him from further questions, but also aware that her story was not one that would be told easily, and he undertook to amuse her with anecdotes about some of the more outrageous characters in the room.

Their time passed pleasantly, and they were soon back at the table with the dreaded water in hand. Anna noticed immediately that Lydia looked fatigued by the noise and bustle of the assembly, and urged her to drink the water quickly so that they could leave.

The baron remained with them and pushed Lydia's chair when they left. At the door they called one of the attendants to summon their carriage, and Anna said regretfully what a shame it was that they should have to ride since it was such a lovely warm day. Lydia, too, looked sad, her comfort materially increased by quitting the loud, dinning hall.

Crewe asked whether he might not be allowed to push Lydia in her chair back to their home. When reminded that it was all the way to the Crescent, he did not demur, but set forth gaily, asking Lydia if she had yet had a building-by-building tour of the city.

She allowed as she had not, and they set off, teasing and

laughing with each other, the baron pushing with steadiness, leaving Anna and Miss Bennet to bring up the rear of their procession.

Along the way Lydia remembered her colt and asked if she might not visit it, since the stable lay on their way. Anna gave her permission, and soon they were standing in the dirty stableyard, a besotted Lydia sitting with her cheek against the muzzle of her colt.

Anna was joined by the baron as they watched.

"She loves that colt."

"Yes, it was one of her greatest losses, losing her pony when she became ill."

"What is the nature of her illness?"

"Indeed, we do not know. Mr. Gibson said there was no sign of disease. He is concerned with her . . . well, he said she did not seem happy."

"She seems very happy."

"Do you think so? Yes, so do I. But I think," she added in fairness, "that he was referring to the deaths of our parents. That perhaps they affected her in some way that destroyed her health."

"That may be. Gibson is a good man and finds things that other physicians often miss. Chiefly, I think, because he takes his patients seriously and attends to what they have to say."

"Oh, yes. He did. He was with Lydie for hours."

"She has improved since I saw her in Yorkshire."

"Oh, do you think so?" Anna turned to him ardently and clutched at his arm, unconsciously pressing herself against him.

Suddenly she drew away, flushed, and looked up into his face. He was watching her with a grave expression, his eyes piercing, his jaw clenched.

Then Anna turned in confusion, drawing away to pat the colt.

"What are you going to name him, Lydie?" she asked.

"Well, with Pamela and Clarissa at home," the baron volunteered, "she must name this one Sir Charles Grandison."

Lydia laughed and wrinkled her nose. "He does not look like a Sir Charles Grandison, does he?"

"Not yet, I am afraid, but he might become grand, you know. You could name him Sir Charles Soon-to-be-Grandison."

She laughed. "What about Charley, for now?"

After watching the colt be led to his stall and given a treat, Lydia allowed herself to be taken home, and before they had quitted the stables, she had fallen asleep with her head resting on the back of the tall chair. When they arrived at their grandmother's house, Anna began to arrange for the footmen to carry her to her chamber, but the baron forestalled her by the simple expedient of picking Lydia up in his arms and carrying her up the tall steps into the hall, where, with a nod from Anna, he climbed the stairs and deposited Lydia on the bed in her chamber, leaving her to the ministrations of her anxious nurse.

When he had returned to the downstairs hall, Anna extended her hand to him. "Thank you for your kindness today, Lord Crewe. I am grateful for your attentions to Lydie and your . . . forbearance toward myself."

"Forbearance. Yes, I would call it forbearance, but I think we would have quite different kinds of forbearance in mind," he said with a wicked grin as he bent over her hand.

He bowed to Miss Bennet and allowed himself to be shown to the door.

As Anna turned away and started toward the library, she passed the door of the drawing room, and her grandmother's voice called out to her.

"Yes, Grandmother," she replied politely as she entered the pale green and gilt room. "How are you today?"

"Come and sit down, child. We have hardly seen anything of each other since you arrived."

Anna obediently did as she was told and waited for her Grandmother to speak.

"You do not give an inch, do you, Anna?"

"I beg your pardon, Grandmother?"

"You are a stiff and proud creature, and I wonder if you are ever planning to forgive me for having neglected you and Lydia."

Anna looked down at her hands in her lap and maintained a silence.

The Countess of Tretham sighed. "Well, perhaps you are as stiff-necked as I was. I never could forgive Edward for marrying that Louisa."

"Louisa was my mother, madam."

"I am well aware she was your mother. You are the spit of her."

Anna's face lit up. "I am?"

"Yes, dear," Lady Tretham said kindly. "You have the identical widow's peak, the same heart-shaped face. And by the way, I approve of your severe hair, Anna. It suits you."

"Thank you, madam."

"But I am not sure about that gown. Surely those shades are rather unusual."

"Yes, I believe they are. I am sorry if you are displeased with my gown."

"Did I say I was displeased, Anna?"

"No, madam. And I wish to thank you again for your generosity. Especially toward Lydie. And for myself, as well. You have been very kind."

"You have to allow me some decent feelings, Anna."

"Of course, madam. Now, if there is nothing else," Anna said, rising.

"Yes. There is a ball tonight at the Rees'. One of the biggest crushes of the summer, I should imagine. Perhaps you would like to attend."

"But surely I was not invited."

"No, but I was, and I think it might be a good time for you to come forward. You have a suitable gown?"

"Yes, thank you, madam. I am tolerably well set up for clothes now."

"Fine. Burleigh sent word that he will be able to attend tonight. He has returned from Dragonsmere, you know, and will accompany us. We will dine quietly here first. Oh, and Anna, who was that man whose voice I heard in the hall just now?"

"Oh, no one, Grandmother, just an acquaintance from Yorkshire."

"I see."

The two women looked at each other, and Anna gave a stiff curtsy and left the room.

Anna sent word that evening that she was not hungry and would have a tray in her chamber as she dressed. The countess thought that perhaps it was due to nerves about her introduction to Bath society.

In fact, Anna's nerves were perfectly under control. She had decided to wear the crimson gown to the ball, the most vivid, eye-catching, spirited gown she had purchased, and she did not intend to be ordered to change it. She planned to descend moments before the carriage was to depart, when the presence of the servants and the lateness of the hour would stay her grandmother's reproofs.

Although Anna was twenty, she had never been to a ball. Her father's ill health and neglect, as well as the absence of a woman in the household to supervise her social life, had meant that she had never even witnessed the bustle and excitement of a household preparing for a lively social gathering.

She laughed as she thought of this, sitting before the window brushing perfume into her hair. *I am probably the oldest girl in all of England to be making my first appearance at a ball this evening*, she thought. But of course, no one would guess it when they saw her scarlet gown.

She lifted it over her head and let it settle over her, wishing that the styles of gowns her mother had worn— the stiff brocades with side panels, the rich fabrics and nipped-in waists—had not gone out of fashion.

Her grandmother had offered her the services of her own lady's maid, but Anna had refused. Even though it was nearly impossible to arrange the pins and tie the tabs by herself, she felt uncomfortable about losing her privacy to her grandmother's spy and certainly did not want any maid's nervous opinions being voiced to her mistress.

She turned this way and that before the looking glass. In truth, she hated these Greek-styled gowns with their shapeless drapery. The gathers under the bosom accentuated her breasts, and Anna ruefully had to admit that the fashion made her look positively overbalanced.

The gown, a sensuous crimson silk, seemed to snake itself around her body. The large, puffed sleeves set off her creamy white bosom. Her auburn hair glowed. Anna reached for a vase of anemones and extracted them one by one, squeezing the stems with a towel, and wove them into her hair, encircling the sinuous bun into which her hair was gathered. She wore no jewels. She had removed the eardrops she had thought to wear—small pendant garnets, because she felt that they detracted from the boldness of the color.

Suddenly she was seized with intense excitement. She was beautiful. She was going to a ball! She was scared to death!

She spun around and threw herself into Lydia's room and pirouetted before her.

"Annie!"

"What do you think, Lydie?"

"Oh, Annie!" Lydia whispered.

"Do you think I will do?"

"Oh, Annie, more than do. You look like a queen."

"Oh, I wish you could come. I will know no one!"

"I would be terrified. Are you terribly nervous?"

"Oh, Lydie." Anna got tears in her eyes. Lydia was such a funny, helpless child, depending on Anna for her support, and yet a wise observer who seldom failed to discern Anna's innermost thoughts. "I am scared to death."

"Good! I am sure I shall be at my first ball. I think it is probably required."

They both giggled, and Anna bent carefully to give her a kiss, then rushed to her room and gathered up her white kid gloves, and then, on an impulse, she left behind the silver-threaded shawl she had laid out to wear. Ballgowns might be worn with spangled, diaphanous shawls, but she knew that hers would be superfluous.

Anna descended the stairs with her head high and allowed her glance to skim the assembled group watching from the hall—her grandmother and maid; Burleigh; the footmen; and Craig, the butler—before focusing sedately on the floor before her.

"Cousin Anna! What are you about! You cannot leave the house attired like that—good God!"

"Hello, Burleigh. How nice to see you again." Anna extended her gloved hand to her cousin, who, red-faced and sputtering, refused it.

"Anna, you are dressed like a Cyprian. Grandmother, do speak to her. She surely cannot understand how she would look to the *ton*—she is too inexperienced. Dear Anna, you will oblige me by changing your gown; otherwise I shall not be able to accompany you to the ball."

"I am sorry, then, that you will not be able to enjoy it with us."

"Anna, I am speaking to you as the head of the family. I order you to return to your chamber and select a gown more suitable to your years and position, and to our family name. I know you do not wish to offend your grandmother or me," he added in a more conciliatory tone.

Anna raised her eyebrows at Burleigh and turned to see what her grandmother would say.

Lady Tretham studied Anna for a long time, from tip to toe, and then spoke only to her maid. "Herndon, please be so good as to go to my chamber and bring down the ruby necklace."

Anna's eyes widened, and she looked at her grandmother, who returned her steady regard but said nothing.

"Grandmother, are you losing your wits? Surely you will not countenance her appearance in that gown."

"Burleigh, I will ask you to keep a civil tongue in your head and remember to whom you speak."

"Forgive me, madam. I am simply concerned. Believe me, I fear you have not been abroad enough to know what a scandal it will cause for her to make an appearance looking like that. Think, Anna. Your grandmother and I know you for the sweet and wonderful girl you are, but to many people here in Bath, you will seem to have burst in upon your grandmother from nowhere, insinuating yourself into her good graces, and spending hundreds of pounds on gowns that will bring scandal to the name of Farrant."

"Oh, Burleigh, you are making too much of a simple gown," Anna said, feeling acutely the justice of what he had said.

"You must face your responsibilities toward your grandmother!"

"Well, I am sure we are glad to hear your opinion, Burleigh," Lady Tretham interjected. "Ah, then, Herndon." She took the necklace from its case and signaled Anna to approach and turn so that she could put the necklace on her.

Anna did so and felt the cold metal against her neck. Her grandmother fastened it and said, "There!" Anna went to the looking glass.

Upon the startling whiteness of her bosom was now set

a long, worked chain of the most delicate gold which ended in a single brilliant ruby set simply in an oval setting, the whole being almost the size of a sovereign. It glowed from the redness of her gown; it glowed like blood against her skin.

She turned back to her grandmother and met her eyes. The barest trace of a smile passed between them.

"But that is the Tretham ruby!" Burleigh exploded. "Anna must not wear it—she is not even married. Only a Tretham bride can be allowed to wear the ruby. But, of course," he added, gaining control of himself, "you do look charming in it. One can almost picture you as a bride, Anna. Now, it might just put thoughts into her head, might it not, Grandmother, not that it is any too soon." He smiled, pleased with himself.

"I think we are ready. Burleigh, do change your mind and come with us. We should so much enjoy the company of a gentleman," Lady Tretham said.

Burleigh hesitated only for a moment and then threw himself toward Anna, offering her his arm and smiling and chatting as though nothing had passed between them. Once they were settled in the carriage, he whispered something to his grandmother which Anna did not hear, for the wheels made a great clatter on the cobbles. She thought it was that he would have to be given charge of Anna, but the prospect was so dismaying she could only hope she misapprehended.

As they ascended the stairs of the grand house where the ball was to take place, the countess tightly held Anna's arm as though she might be intending to slip away. Anna found it comforting, a fact that surprised her. All the while her grandmother kept up a steady flow of conversation although Anna was much too keyed up to make sensible responses.

"This will be a much smaller ball than if it were in London, of course, only a hundred or so guests. Ah, there is Lady Johnson. How nice to see her. She was so ill last year. And Lord Jones. Oh, mercy, look at that woman in white over there. Why, she must be forty if she is a day, in a gown meant for a girl!" And so it went until suddenly they were inside and at the top of a grand staircase being presented to a row of people whose names were lost to Anna's distracted excitement.

She was swept into the ballroom, where glittering candles, festoons of flowers, the scents of the ladies and the blossoms, the heat, and the music all conspired to bring a sudden rush of color to Anna's face and an intense light to her eyes. She turned slowly and took it all in as though she had never seen its like before. As indeed, she had not.

The countess looked over at her and laughed. "You are gawking, Anna."

"Of course I am gawking—this is my first ball!"

"Your first ball?"

Anna looked at her levelly. "Yes. This is my first ball. And," she said, her eyes lighting with pleasure on the garlands of greens woven between the long windows, "it promises to be a very beautiful one."

Anna's grandmother watched her for a moment and set her jaw, took firm hold of Anna's arm, and began a circuit of the room, making introductions as she went.

About a half hour later Anna had recovered her customary aplomb, and it was soon borne in on her, as her quivering excitement subsided, that she was indeed making a stir both in her own right and as the unknown granddaughter of the formidable countess. Wherever she glanced in the room, she saw that people were watching her and talking.

All but Burleigh, who did not seem to know what to do. He could not very well expostulate with Anna or her grandmother in public, yet to be seen in her immediate company was to countenance his cousin's shocking behavior. But again, to remove himself from them was impossible as he dare not affront his grandmother.

So he remained with them, positioning himself at his grandmother's ear, maintaining a whispered commentary to the effect that although they knew that Anna was a young woman of impeccable virtue, no one in Bath knew that, and perhaps she had been too indulgent with her; perhaps he should be allowed to undertake her supervision. Would she notice how the women were whispering behind their fans about her, and although Anna was not as high in the instep as she looked, nor truly immodest, yet, with proper handling by him she might . . .

Anna was unaware of the undercurrent, concentrating on taking in every face and trying to attach and remember the correct names. She was also making a mental list of families who said they had daughters about Lydia's age. She mentioned to her grandmother the need for suitable companions for Lydia, and her grandmother, nodding and trying to move away from Burleigh's sibilant whispering, issued invitations on Lydia's behalf.

Suddenly she heard her grandmother cry, "Why, Horace, what are you doing in town? You rogue. Do you not know that when you come to Bath you are supposed to pay your compliments to one of your mother's dearest friends?"

Anna turned as slowly as she could command herself to do and looked straight into the eyes of Horace Crewe, whose gaze moved slowly down her body, taking in the ruby, the whiteness of her bosom, the shocking boldness of her gown, and her beauty—her absolute, unparalleled, dazzling beauty. With an effort he brought his gaze back to hers and bowed politely.

"Enchanted."

Chapter Twelve

"*AND GEORGE IVES*, is it not?" added the countess. "I have not seen your grandmother in an age."

"Your service, Lady Tretham." The stranger, a young man as blond as Horace Crewe was dark, and stocky where the older man was lean, bent over the countess' hand and then turned appreciatively to Anna and bowed over hers.

"Ives?" asked Anna. "Are you related to the Iveses of Lynthorpe Hall?"

"Why, yes, that is my home."

"Really!" said Anna, at that moment realizing how awkward a line of conversation this could become.

"Yes, are you familiar with the place?"

"I was employed there."

"Employed there?" said the handsome young man, frowning. "I am sorry, but I do not understand."

"I was a companion to your grandmother."

"Oh, yes, Anna! I remember the name. Anna Smith, thought . . ."

"Well, yes, it is confusing . . . but yes, I am the same. How pleasant to meet you, Mr. Ives."

"I only wish I had met you sooner."

"Well, George," the baron interjected, "I can only imagine that it is because you did not drive out often enough. Now I, for one, could hardly venture onto the roads of Yorkshire without running straight into Lady Anna."

Anna laughed, and Horace related the incidents to George and the countess. Continuing, he said, "And I was delighted to make Lady Anna's acquaintance under vastly more auspicious circumstances yesterday when I was allowed to escort her home from the Pump Room."

Anna glanced at her grandmother, who realized that it had been Horace's voice she had heard in the hall. "Well, Horace, I am doubly offended then, for not only have you not called on me, but you were in my home and did not bother to speak a word to me."

"You will forgive me, Lady Tretham. It is an oversight I will rectify tomorrow, if I may."

"Of course, Horace. How amazing that you should have your father's looks as you do. By Heaven, was I in love with him! And so was your grandmother, George, no matter how she might deny it."

At that moment Burleigh, making one of his darts at the punch table, returned in time to be asked to juggle his glass while being introduced to Horace and George. Horace Crewe he knew by reputation as an excellent whip, a cunning gamester, a man of the *ton*, and one of the richest men in England. It was almost enough to instill dislike.

Anna performed the introductions.

"Crewe!" Burleigh exclaimed. "What are you doing in Bath? I would have thought Bath dull sport for you."

"Well, Tretham! So you two are related," he said, looking from Burleigh to Anna.

"Yes, we are cousins," Anna answered.

"Indeed we are," Burleigh added, possessively taking Anna's elbow. "And a troublesome cousin she is, too. The little puss showed up from nowhere and seems determined to set Bath on its ear. But we have had a nice talk this evening, have we not, and as head of the family I have been able to set you straight about the ways of the *ton*, haven't I, puss?"

Anna smiled without meeting Crewe's eyes.

The music began, and Burleigh claimed her for the first dance. She was determined to be pleasant and reassure him enough as to her character that he would abandon his criticism. She certainly wanted no more patronizing scenes like the one he had just enacted.

"Burleigh, are you any more disposed to my presence here than you were?" she asked in one of the intervals when the dance brought them together. "Please say you are," she added with a teasing smile.

Burleigh saw the flirtatious look and preened. "Of course I am, my dear—your charms have won me over. But you must allow yourself to be guided by me. Think of yourself as fortunate to have an older, wiser cousin to lead you into the intricacies of society."

"Goodness, Burleigh, you make yourself sound ancient. But I have my grandmother for that."

"You know how I feel about your imposing on your grandmother, Anna," Burleigh said as sternly as he could while hopping and twirling to the music.

Anna smiled to herself. Beads of perspiration stood out on his forehead, but the effort to dance and talk at the same time did not deter him.

"I will always try to be guided by you, Burleigh, but you must allow me small things like choosing my gowns. In the larger things, however . . ."

Burleigh stopped for a moment, panting, and spoke with feeling. "Yes, it is just those larger things, Anna, I hope, that is, I intend . . . there is something . . ."

He was forced to discontinue his efforts to speak by the requirements of the quadrille. When they came together again, Anna asked him about Crewe.

"Crewe!" Burleigh said with a snort. "A conceited man, high in the instep, and his reputation with women is disgraceful. I can not imagine a man whose friendship could do you more positive harm, Anna. He is not suitable for a Farrant."

"Grandmother seems to like him."

"Your grandmother is opinionated and eccentric, guided by the loose morals of an earlier, less discriminating age. You must turn to me on such issues and not rely on your grandmother's view of what is proper. Why, look at her acquiescence in allowing you to wear that gown and giving you the ruby to wear to an insignificant ball! It passes understanding."

Anna valiantly tried to change the subject and found that only by flirting could she deter Burleigh from his tendency to pontificate. It was her first dance at her first ball, and she was disappointed that it was devoid of charm. Indeed, she found dancing with Burleigh fatiguing and was glad when she was free of him.

He returned her to the countess and left to refill his glass. Her eyes were still on him when she heard another's voice and looked over to find that Crewe was watching her, his hand extended. She was on the floor with him and in his arms before she realized he had asked her for a waltz!

She had never waltzed. She and Jenny Pleasance, her best friend in Berkshire, had practiced all the dances when they were girls and had made a few clumsy attempts to master the steps, but the shocking reputation that clung to the dance had not been sufficient inducement to overcome their awkwardness.

"Oh!" she cried in dismay. "I have never waltzed!"

"You do not know how to waltz?" Horace asked, holding her in his arms and smiling down at her.

"No. Oh, please, may we sit this one out?"

"No. Come. It is time you learned. We can move to the side where you can trip away without doing anyone the kind of harm you do when driving a cart."

"Oh, dear, I . . ." Anna was so distracted by her embarrassment that she failed to hear the teasing.

He began to move rhythmically to the intoxicating music and held her so firmly in his arms that she had no choice but to move her body in time with his.

"One two three, one two three, one two three . . ."

"I can count!" she hissed.

"That is the rhythm. Stop." She stopped perforce when he stopped. He looked at her with laughter lighting his eyes and struggled to keep from smiling. "Now, just relax. It is one two three, understand, and you turn as you do the steps."

"Please, people are watching us."

"I daresay they are. You are the most beautiful woman here and wearing the season's most shocking gown."

Anna stiffened, and he laughed. "One who wears such a gown should be able to withstand the comment it causes. Now," he said, raising his eyebrows against her response, "let us begin again."

Anna struggled not to disgrace herself, but she seemed to have a fatal impulse to tend left when Lord Crewe was tending right, to be stepping away from him when he was stepping away from her, and once when she recovered and stepped forward, so did he and they collided with a shocking impact. Anna stood stunned and looked up at him, and he, just as still, looked down at her until he said, hoarsely, "I think we had better leave waltzing lessons for another day."

Anna averted her face and nodded, and as they strolled from the dance floor, she kept it so. He led them onto a piazza which extended to a garden down a long sloping hill that beckoned many couples into the lovely summer night.

She stood near a wide flower-filled urn, drinking in the air, enjoying the quiet.

He broke the silence. "You are very beautiful."

She looked at him wordlessly.

He suddenly laughed. "What an odd woman you are. You dress like a Cyprian and act like a girl attending her first ball."

Anna smiled ruefully. "That is what my cousin said."

"What?"

"That I look like a Cyprian. Is it really so simple in society to look immoral? Simply by wearing a scarlet gown? What a rigid world it is."

"Yes, that is true," he said thoughtfully. "But that does not explain why you cannot waltz."

"My lord, you were absolutely correct. This is my first ball." She looked at him defiantly.

He could see her braced against slight and forbore to comment. "Burleigh is your cousin. He is now the present Earl of Tretham, am I right?"

"Yes."

"He just acceded to the title, in the last few years?"

"Yes."

"You are not very helpful."

"Why should I satisfy your curiosity?"

"Politeness, my dear. Politeness usually requires that a man and woman getting to know each other at a ball ask a string of foolish questions which they answer so that their own foolish questions will be answered."

"Well, then, I need not answer you because I have no foolish questions of my own."

"Touché."

Anna grinned. Then she sighed. "My father was the sixth earl. He died five years ago. My cousin Burleigh inherited the title and my—our home, Dragonsmere, in Berkshire."

"Dragonsmere . . ."

"Do you know it?"

"Who does not know it? A Norman keep is the foundation of its structure, am I right?"

"Yes."

"You lost Dragonsmere."

"Please, Lord Crewe, we need not discuss this further."

"And when I met you, you were living in such dire want, in that miserable hovel."

"My lord, please."

"Good God, no wonder you stole my stickpin."

"I . . . !"

"I am surprised you did not steal all my jewels. It must be that you simply did not know the extent of my collection— I have quite an array, you know. Some especially fine sapphires worked into the most cunning buttons. And if you had seen my ruby shirt studs . . . or . . ."

"Please, my lord," said Anna, giggling, "this is not at all proper."

"What, you do not find an inventory of my possessions to be a proper topic of conversation? I am devastated. Am I to assume that you would no more be charmed by a list of my racers, my residences, my carriages . . ."

"Oh, stop, please, you are ridiculous."

"I, ridiculous. And you, sublime."

She laughed again. "I must return. I have promised the next dance to George Ives."

"We will continue at our next dance, then." Winking outrageously, he took his leave.

Anna was in high spirits when George Ives found her and led her in a country dance which she acquitted with grace and spirit that caught the attention of those who were not dancing, and she could not resist sending a look of triumph toward the baron, who held his glass aloft in response.

When she went to supper, Anna was seated with her grandmother, Burleigh, George Ives, and Horace Crewe, whom her grandmother continued to berate about his inattention to her, a subject that allowed them to brangle and spar, an activity they both seemed to enjoy. George sat next to Anna, and they spoke quietly about Mrs. Ives; George making it clear that he was every bit as fond of her as she had been of him.

The teasing voice of Burleigh cut into their conversation. "Now tell me, Anna, just how many gowns have you purchased since coming to Bath?"

Anna smiled pleasantly, hoping her embarrassment did not show. Conversation at their table ceased.

Finding encouragement in her silence, he continued, making use of a jocular tone that implied a much more intimate relationship between them than obtained. "I hear that you bought out Madame Fouchon, is that true?"

"She is a wonderful dressmaker," Anna said evenly.

"Twenty-seven gowns, I understand."

"Why, Burleigh, how could you have heard such a figure?"

"Ah, so you do not deny it. These women," he said, with an elbow in Crewe's side, "they cannot stop spending money even when it is not theirs. Can you, Coz?"

Anna flushed and looked away.

"You are fortunate to have a grandmother as generous as yours," Burleigh said with a bow to his grandmother.

Anna answered. "In fact, Burleigh, she has not nearly been generous enough." When the countess stiffened, Anna went on, "I wanted to buy an ermine cloak reversing to sable, and I saw the most lovely pair of sapphire eardrops which I most particularly wanted, and there was a coach-and-eight—all white, you know—with fourteen outriders, but she would say no." Her mouth turned down in mock sadness.

"Well, naturally she would say no," Burleigh sputtered, and then grew angry when the others at the table burst out laughing.

When he realized he had been the butt of a joke, he adopted a teasing tone which Anna felt was a heroic effort on his part to tamp down a fierce and sudden rage. *But surely,* she thought to herself, *I must be wrong.*

He spoke with a braying laugh. "These women, they create outrageous burdens by their extravagance and then charm their way out of the consequences! But that is what we love them for, is it not?"

He sat back with a satisfied look on his face, gazing at Anna, admiring her high color, content to watch her and dream of the future.

The supper ended with constraint, and Anna looked forward to the dances that remained. She danced again with George, who was charming and seemed as pleased by their previous if unknown link as he was by her beauty. In fact, he was quite head over heels in love with her in a pleasantly boyish way. Anna was touched and saw much in the kindness of his manner that reminded her of his grandmother.

When Horace came to claim a schottische, Anna refused to meet his eyes and chatted determinedly on general topics.

"How do you like the weather in Bath, my lord? Do you not find it unusually salubrious? I do. I find it quite salubrious."

"Do you? Salubrious, find it salubrious?"

"Yes, very, and you?"

"Well, *salubrious* is a fine word, but I would say, rather, chilly."

"Chilly?"

"Do you not think it has been unaccountably chilly in Bath?"

"Well, chilly? I do not know. It certainly has not been overly warm. I would not say that it has been warm."

"Oh, Lady Anna, spare me more of this foolishness. I do not care a fig about the weather, and I doubt you do, either."

Anna flushed and bit her lip.

"There, I have hurt your feelings. I am sorry."

"You have not hurt my feelings," she said through clenched teeth.

"Oh, I thought I had. And I would have been very sorry—devastated to have hurt your feelings. Hurting your feelings is something I would be loath to do. Of all the things I would be loath to do, hurting your feelings would be first."

"Oh, stop it, or I shall kick you!"

"Ah, Lady Anna, I do bring out the best in you, do I not?"

The dance separated them, and Anna felt completely in control again when they rejoined hands.

"Now, then, where were we?" he asked.

"You were telling me what you were doing in Bath."

"Was I? What a poor memory I have! Such a Tragedy in One So Young, do you not think so?"

"In Bath, doing."

"Whiling away the time before I go to London, where I shall while away the time before I go to Hampshire, or perhaps it is Scotland I am waiting to go to, to shoot grouse. Or is that in January?"

"Are you never serious?" she inquired.

"I am serious. I am trying to convey the somewhat, shall we say, randomness of my life."

"It sounds terrible."

"My life?"

"Yes."

The figures of the dance separated them again. Anna went through the paces automatically, eager to continue the conversation—if that is what it could be called—with the infuriating and absolutely riveting man who partnered her.

"Ready?" he asked when they came together.

"Ready?"

"For our next sparring match?"

Chapter
Thirteen

ANNA'S LAUGH WAS so ringing and clear that all those in
their set turned to her. She did not notice, for her shining
eyes were fixed on Lord Crewe. He had noticed, as he had
noticed everything she had done since first entering the
ballroom gaping like a young girl. He had taken in the
women's disapproval of her attire, the men's fascination;
he had taken in how her ease, grace, and address had won
over the women, and her beauty, gaiety, and energy had
won the hearts of the men. Oh, he had noticed.

"My lord, you wrong me. Indeed, I do not wish to
spar with you. My sole goal is to acquit myself in this
conversation with all possible decorum and civility."

"Decorum and civility—just the words I would have
used."

Again a giggle broke from Anna. "You know, I cannot
be serious in your presence even for a moment."

"I am honored."

"Yet I judge you a very serious man."

"Entirely."

"Oh, well. I shall have to restrict my conversations to Lydie from now on. She is sensible."

"You love Lydie, don't you?"

Anna stumbled in the execution of her steps, and her eyes clouded over. "Why do you ask that?"

"It has occurred to me that you would do anything for her."

She looked at him steadily. There was kindness in his eyes, and something else, something piercing and unyielding.

"Yes."

"Anything at all?"

"Anything at all."

The dance ended soberly, and sadly Anna turned away. Crewe caught her arm and turned her gently about. "No, after an evening of such sparkling conversation, such epigrammatic sayings, such pithy truths, I cannot allow you to walk away looking ready to cry."

Anna stood defenselessly, set to abide whatever nonsense he would choose to indulge in. Instead he let the silence grow between them, surrounding them, protecting them from the rest of the world. Anna watched him within the island they made and knew that she wanted to be in his arms, to feel his body against hers. And so she moved away because there was nothing she could possibly say or do that would not give away what she felt.

By two in the morning Lady Tretham insisted they leave. Anna was only too willing. Since the second dance with Crewe she had been tormented by a longing to be alone. And finally, when she reached home and the solitude of her bed, it developed that all she wanted to do was cry.

Anna slept late, indulging in the pleasure of awakening only to fall back to sleep again. Finally she rose, impelled by the desire to tell Lydia about the ball.

They shared Lydia's breakfast from a tray, and Anna described the ballroom, the flowers, the gowns and headdresses, the dancing and the supper, omitting all the unaccountable things that had passed between Crewe and herself. Lydia was enchanted and laughed with delight and asked so many questions that Anna did not think there was a wall sconce undescribed by the time she was satisfied. She was delighted with the story of the luckless waltz and made Anna promise to have in a dancing master so Lydia could watch and learn it, too.

After leaving her sister to her exercise, Anna descended to seek out her grandmother, to thank her for the ball, and to discuss her plans to expand Lydia's circle of friends.

When she went into the empty drawing room she noticed a huge vase of deep-wine-colored roses standing on a table before the window. Anna was enthralled. So many flowers—there were forty at least! She had no idea that her grandmother was so extravagant. Perhaps she was planning a reception that she had not told her of.

Anna stood over them, breathing in their scent, when a voice caught her by surprise.

"Do you like them?"

Horace Crewe stood in the doorway.

"They are beautiful."

"I am glad."

"You are glad?"

"I am glad you like them."

"But why should I not like them? They are very beautiful."

"Why should I not be glad you like them?"

"I really do not think I understand you."

"Nor I you."

"Perhaps we are fated never to understand each other."

"It certainly seems that way."

"Let us begin again," Anna said. "Good morning, Lord Crewe, I was admiring the lovely roses my grandmother placed here. Are they not quite amazingly beautiful?"

"Ah, that is the problem. It was not your grandmother who had them placed there. It was me."

"You! But why should you be sent to purchase the flowers for my grandmother's reception?"

"Is your grandmother planning a reception?"

"I do not know, but I assume so, or she would not have purchased quite so many flowers."

"She did not purchase them. I did."

"Yes, and that is what I cannot understand."

"Lady Anna," the baron said, seizing her shoulders without ceremony. "Stop."

Turning her slightly within his right arm so that she was pressed against his chest, he reached sideways toward the flowers and among the blossoms found a long piece of paper folded over and sealed with wax, which he handed to her.

She stood within his embrace, her head resting against his chest. She read, "Lady Anna Farrant."

She slipped her finger under the wax and broke the seal. Something wrapped in gold tissue fell out; she held it between her fingers and read the note.

"To Anna, the Rose of Bath. My first tribute. Horace Crewe."

Anna blushed but did not move from the circle of his arm. His second arm came around to rest on her shoulders. She was aware of his hands.

She opened the gold tissue and folded it back to see what it held. It was the stickpin.

Carefully, so that his hands would not brush against her body, she ducked from under his embrace, the stickpin in her palm.

"This is yours."

"Keep it, Anna. I want you to have it."

"I have no right to it. It is a symbol of something shameful to me. You know that I would have kept it if I could have got away with it. I stole it and would have sold it for money."

"I know," he said gently, looking at the jewel in her palm. "You stole it because you were desperate for money, for Lydia."

"That does not excuse it."

"Yes, it does. Anna, I want you to have it because it is what brought us together. But especially I want you to have it, to give it to you as a symbol of everything that I would like to give you."

"Anna!"

Anna and Horace jerked apart and spun around to encounter a red-faced Burleigh coming into the room through the open door of the adjoining parlor. "Anna, explain yourself!"

Anna, shaken, was unable to speak without a betraying tremble. "You have no right to speak to me that way."

Horace held out his hand placatingly. "It is my fault, Lord Tretham. I was told by Craig that Lady Anna was in here. I had no idea she would be alone."

Burleigh chose to be mollified and forced an unconvincing smile. "Oh, that is quite all right. It is just that I wish to speak privately with Anna, if you do not mind."

He looked impatiently at Crewe, who had no choice but to leave, despite the invitation he read in Anna's eyes. He bent over her hand, bowed to Burleigh, and left.

Burleigh and Anna waited in silence until the door closed behind them. Then they both spoke at once.

"Anna, you must avoid that man . . ."

"Burleigh, that was insufferably rude . . ."

They broke off, both too furious to be civil.

At last Burleigh remembered his purpose in coming to find Anna, a purpose he had almost sacrificed to his outrage at finding her in a compromising situation with Crewe.

"Anna, come, sit down. Let us forget our arguments. Come."

He led her to damask-covered chairs before the window, Anna allowing herself to be led.

They sat. Anna wore a gown the color of apricots and with the sun shining on her, she radiated a glowing warmth that took Burleigh's breath away. He, attired almost exclusively in bright lime green, offered a less inspiring vision. His girth forced him to sit with his knees wide apart—his tight clothes forced him to upright rigidity.

Anna tried to suppress the uncharitable thoughts his appearance prompted, but it was hard to do so given her impatience with his overbearing intrusion into her life after years of neglect.

"What is it, Burleigh?"

"Are you happy in Bath, Cousin?"

Anna thought. "I really do not know, Burleigh. It is not a question I have yet considered."

"I thought as much, Cousin. You live with no regard for tomorrow, for the future. Lydia is improving every day, and when she is well, what will you do? *No*," he said, gesturing for her to remain silent. "You are living now at your grandmother's expense, but that cannot go on forever. You must have asked yourself how long she would be willing to keep you, can she afford to keep you."

Again he raised his hand against her speaking. It seemed to Anna as though he had prepared a speech which he must perform exactly as he had memorized it, without interruption.

"Anna, I am not a wealthy man, but I have managed my inheritance well and I am pleased with the restoration of Dragonsmere. I think if you could see it you would think it more prosperous than it was in your father's day.

"I am at the time in my life when I wish to marry, and I can do so now that my affairs are in order.

"Anna, I ask you to do me the honor of becoming my wife. Return to Dragonsmere—with Lydia if you choose.

In marrying me, you will find security without having to depend on your grandmother."

Anna had grown more and more astonished as the direction of Burleigh's discourse became clear. She was caught completely off guard.

"I . . . I hardly know what to say. It is very generous of you to be concerned with my and Lydie's welfare. I know how anxious you are about Grandmother and my not imposing on her. I think we differ on that, for I do not see our presence here an undue burden. She is very wealthy, is she not?"

Burleigh hesitated, as if reluctant to speak. "Yes, she once had a great deal . . . but . . ."

"But what?"

"I have the privilege and burden, Anna, of understanding her situation, and I am sorry to have to tell you that in a few years she will be in great difficulty financially."

"My heavens! Have you told her? Can you help her?"

"I am trying, Anna. One way is in this, by taking charge of you and Lydia, to take these burdens, at least, from her hands. You have not answered me."

"No, I have not. You have put me in an uncomfortable position. Knowing what you have told me makes me realize that I must not be a burden to her, and yet I need security for Lydie, but . . . but what you propose is not really a marriage. It is a financial arrangement. We hardly know each other and have no feelings . . ."

"But we are cousins, are we not? Between us there can be no illusions. We love each other in the best way, with the trust and constancy of family members. The other love will grow, and as for me, I find you very beautiful."

Anna shifted uneasily in her seat. "It is true that we are united by kinship, but can that be enough? I . . . I believe I must love where I marry."

"You do not have that choice, Anna."

"But of course I do, everyone does. To marry where there is love or not to marry at all."

"No, in your case the choice is to marry me or to lose what little security your grandmother is still able to give you. It may even be necessary for her to ask you to leave."

"I must risk it, then." Anna rose.

Burleigh struggled to his feet. "Surely you do not mean to turn down my offer." He laughed. "You do not have any choice!"

"But I do have a choice," Anna said quietly. "I choose not to marry you. But I am deeply grateful for the honor you have done . . ."

"Anna, you cannot refuse me!"

"But I have."

Burleigh stared, his face suffusing with color. He had not considered a refusal. He stepped close and shouted into her face, "You will accept me. You will!"

"I am sorry, Burleigh, but I must refuse. The circumstances . . ."

He was not listening. "You shall, Anna, you shall come begging to me. Just you wait!"

Anna backed away in horror. Fury had him in its grip. Spittle gleamed on his lips. His eyes were pinpoints of black, his hands convulsively clutched at her.

She eluded him and fled from the room.

She slammed the door of her bedchamber and ran to the window to gulp fresh air as though to cleanse herself of pollution. She pressed her hands to her temples and closed her eyes.

Had Crewe been going to propose to her? Surely he had been. Oh, yes!

She spun around the room hugging herself, full of joy and happiness. Certainly, the next time she saw him . . . But the prospect was too wonderful even to imagine. No imagining could contain the full measure of happiness his offer would bring.

She threw herself on the bed. Her eyes were closed, a smile played on her lips. She dreamed of Horace Crewe.

The scene with Burleigh was quite forgotten.

Anna was brought out of her reverie by Lydia's knocking. The girl struck a pose in the doorway and then entered, laughing, to display a new figured muslin gown.

Anna was still not used to Lydia's new strength, to the fact that she found it possible to dress herself, care for her pets, and perform the daily tasks that had heretofore been performed by herself or Miss Bennet.

"Yes, you look very pretty," Anna said, laughing. "And you are becoming vain!"

"And you look absolutely beautiful. What have you been thinking about with that odd smile on your face? Certainly not our excursion to Sydney Gardens!"

Anna laughed and twirled about. "Ah, yes, Sydney Gardens! Oh, what bliss, what joy! Oh! Let us go to Sydney Gardens!"

She grabbed Lydia's hands and spun her around.

Lydia was startled and breathless and fell onto Anna's bed laughing. "Oh, Annie," she said and then, unaccountably, burst into tears.

Immediately contrite, Anna dropped down beside her and took her hands. "Lydie, what is it?"

"Oh, Annie." Lydia sobbed into Anna's shoulder.

Anna sat still until Lydia could control herself.

"Do you know how good it is to be able to romp?" And on the word *romp* she fell into sobbing again and was soon joined by Anna.

Then, just as suddenly, they both started to giggle and fell into helpless laughter.

It was thus that Miss Bennet found them and was forced to suppress the impulse to correct their hoydenish behavior. She was not sure she would ever be able to correct any excesses that resulted from Lydia's high spirits.

The girls became aware of her presence and tried to restrain themselves. They were simultaneously disheveled and radiant.

After lunch and a brief rest for Lydia, they set out on their excursion to the pleasure gardens behind the Sydney Hotel. Lydia was pushed into the garden in her chair but left it and walked to a low bench beneath some trees, where they both sat, playing with their parasols and looking about at the strollers with every expectation of pleasant diversion.

They made a lovely picture, one demure in white, the other glowing in rose and copper. Pale and vivid. The younger girl animated and chatting, the older one sedate and quiet.

"Anna, you are not listening to a thing I am saying."

"Of course I am, dear."

"Well, what did I say?"

"That I am not listening."

"No, before that."

"Oh, Lydie, you are right," Anna said, laughing. "Tell me again."

"I was asking you what Lord Crewe looked like in his ball dress."

"Quite pleasant."

"Quite pleasant," Lydia scoffed. "Oh, look," she said, nodding toward a path to their right. "Do you see that blond man—oh, Annie! He is coming this way!"

"Lady Anna."

"Mr. Ives! How nice to see you. Lydie, this is Mr. George Ives, who grew up at Lynthorpe Hall, of all places. We met last night. His grandmother is Mrs. Ives. My sister, Lady Lydia Farrant."

"I had no idea that two such lovely women lived in my neighborhood. Why did I never hear of you?"

"Well, I have been ill," Lydia said, blushing.

"My sister is in Bath to recover her health, Mr. Ives."

"I would think, looking at her, that she was glowing with health," he said, glowing himself with admiration for her.

"It is true that Bath has been very kind to her," Anna said, amused.

"Would you like to try some ices, Lady Anna, Lady Lydia?"

"Oh, please call me Lydia."

"We should love some ices, Mr. Ives."

The young man left and returned shortly with three lemon ices. For a while he knelt awkwardly before them, until Anna noticed a woman she had met the evening before and rose to greet her. Then the young man, not taking his eyes off Lydia, appropriated Anna's seat as she had assumed he would.

Anna chatted with the matron, who invited Anna to visit with her daughter. Anna ended the conversation by bringing the matron forward to introduce her to Lydia. Lydia and Mr. Ives were deep in a conversation about Herodotus, who turned out to be a great mutual love, and Anna, more amused than astonished, waited while they quoted passages to each other. "Lydie, love, I hate to interrupt you, but Mrs. Petry would like to make your acquaintance."

Anna performed the introductions, and George Ives leapt from his seat to allow the older woman to sit down. The latter was plainly charmed by Lydia and impressed by the Latin she had heard and the young girl's manners. "I think you could be a good influence on my Meggy," she told her "She is just a bit wild, in love with nothing but clothes and her horse."

Lydia burst out, "Oh, and I hope she will be a good influence on me, making me a bit more wild and encouraging me to ride all day and change my gowns ten times a day!"

They all laughed. Anna would have liked to leave when Mrs. Petry did, but George had resumed his seat. Soon he and Lydia were deep into mutual recitations. She did not have the heart to interrupt.

She wandered off and was pleased to encounter Caroline Wilcox, a young woman she had previously met. As they traversed the Labyrinth, each considered the other with uneasy suspicion. Lady Tretham had called Caroline something of a bluestocking, and Caroline thought Anna so beautiful and exotic she did not expect a sensible word from her.

They were both pleasantly surprised. Neither turned out to be as formidable as the other had feared, and they shared a love of reading and horses. Anna had not ridden since her days at Dragonsmere, and Caroline promised the loan of one of her horses if she would go riding with her the next morning.

It was with the happy satisfaction of having made new friends that Anna and Lydia returned to the tall house in the center of the Crescent. They entered quietly, both of them preoccupied and alone with private thoughts.

Horace Crewe's presence took them by surprise. Lydia immediately welcomed him with open pleasure. Anna alternately paled and flushed. She could hardly bring herself to look at him.

Crewe, who had been closeted with their grandmother in the back parlor, greeted them warmly, scarcely taking his eyes off Anna.

Lydia, noting this, directed a footman to help her to her room. Blushing furiously, Anna entered the front parlor whose door Horace held open for her. She thought she glimpsed Burleigh at the top of the stairs but was too happy to think of him and his awkward, unwelcome proposal.

Horace closed the door softly behind her and, without words, held open his arms to her, and she walked into his embrace.

They held each other with feelings made up of both peace and the deep unease of passion.

Suddenly the door burst open, and Burleigh rushed into the room. He did not pause to react to the embrace he discovered.

"Anna! The ruby has been stolen! What have you done with it?"

Chapter
Fourteen

ANNA STEPPED BACK. "Ruby . . . stolen? Burleigh, what are you talking about?"

"The Tretham ruby you wore last night. Where is it?"

"But I told you at lunch, remember? I told Grandmother that I had put it in the blue leather box on my dresser. No doubt Herndon took it and returned it to Grandmother's room."

"Yes, that is what you said, but when she went to get it, it was not there."

"It was not in my box?"

"No."

Anna was aware that Horace had stepped away from her, as though to detach himself from the confusion. She forced herself not to look at him and made an effort to respond calmly, without panicking.

"Burleigh, have you spoken with Herndon?"

"Of course. She said there was nothing in that box but a string of pearls, some cheap stone necklaces, and some silver eardrops."

"Well, yes," Anna said, feeling her face flush, "that is an accurate inventory of my jewels. I shall speak to her."

Anna looked toward Crewe, who stood against the mantel inspecting his fingernails. He shot a look at Burleigh while she watched him, then looked back at his hand. She wondered if he was purposely avoiding meeting her eye.

"Will you excuse me, please?" she said, approaching and facing him squarely. "I must look into this."

"Of course," he said. He bowed over her hand, but by no special look or pressure on her fingers could she discern comfort or reassurance. They parted as though strangers.

Anna found Herndon, Lady Tretham's dresser, who verified what Burleigh had said. After lunch her mistress had told her to retrieve the ruby from Anna's box and return it to its accustomed place in her dressing room. When Herndon had looked in Anna's room, the ruby was missing.

Anna went then to her room and searched it thoroughly, knowing it would be futile since she was certain she had not misplaced it. But searching gave her something to do and kept unwelcome thoughts at bay.

Finally she sought out her grandmother, but she was resting, and Anna returned to her room alone, with no explanation given—not yet understood, not yet forgiven.

She rested and called for her supper on a tray and ate with Lydia. Lydia, who knew nothing about the ruby, was nonetheless subdued as well. Miss Bennet carried the conversation, which neither girl attended to. They ate quietly, and then Anna returned to her room to prepare for the evening.

Attired in a gown of copper satin, the color of her hair when the light glistened on it, and bedecked with violet roses on both her gown and in her hair, Anna wished for a fleeting moment that she were wearing something decorous, some delicate white confection that would proclaim innocence and virtue. But it was too late to regret

her choices. She had wanted to be noticed, and noticed
she would be.

In the hallway her grandmother greeted her cordially
and did not speak of the missing ruby. Burleigh ignored
her, fussing over Lady Tretham's shawl. He did not even
bother to chastise her, although his knotted brow spoke of
his disapproval of her raiment. The countess merely nodded
to her, and then, as if an afterthought, said, "You look well
tonight, Anna."

Anna threw her a surprised, grateful glance and sketched
a curtsy. They departed together in the carriage to attend a
small dancing party at the home of one of Lady Tretham's
friends about three miles outside the city.

It was a soft night, still light although nearly ten o'clock.
Nearing midsummer, the nights were magic, holding an
opalescent light that never quite faded before brightening
again into day. Anna missed the longer hours of light
in Yorkshire, but enjoyed the balmy, gentle night air of
Avon.

They arrived at the mansion-house, a Queen Anne structure that gleamed in the middle of its wide park like polished silver. There were not as many carriages or people
for this ball, and the house, when they climbed the stairs
to the public rooms, easily accommodated the guests who
moved among the rooms, laughing and chatting.

Anna looked wistfully at them, so gay and untroubled.
She stood demurely with her grandmother, speaking little
to the many people who greeted her grandmother as they
made their way into the ballroom.

Immediately her eyes discovered Horace Crewe, standing
before a beautiful woman with midnight black hair and
black eyes, whose small stature made her seem a frail exotic, like a Spanish infanta washed up on English soil. Anna
looked away, turning to an old cavalier her grandmother
was in conversation with, and gave him such a magnificent
smile that the old man's blood warmed, and he impulsively

asked her to dance, although he had forsworn dancing years before.

Anna allowed him to lead her out, not caring whom she danced with, and her evening passed in just such an uncaring way. She danced with old men and young men, with married men and single men who fought to arouse her interest. She dipped and bowed, spun and curtsied, swayed and leapt with the music, her radiant rustling gown catching the light, her hair gleaming in the brilliant light of the chandeliers, her smile dazzling those who watched her. Indeed, everyone watched her.

Everyone but Horace Crewe. When the company went down for supper, Anna was escorted by George Ives, who had been paying court to her, but since his conversation was exclusively about Lydia, it was no mystery where his thoughts lay. She was delighted with his company—anyone who loved her sister would be himself loved—but she did not hesitate to gently point out that her sister was but sixteen.

As they made their way to the supper table and took their places, George earnestly said he understood that, that he was leaving for an extended trip to the Continent in September—now that the war was over and it was possible to travel again—and that when he returned, in a year or so, perhaps he then might pay court to her. Anna pressed his hand and said that would be delightful. He then asked her for permission to write to Lydia, and after reminding him that time can change all plans and feelings, she gave it willingly.

George Ives provided peaceful and soothing company, and the other men who had joined her party with her grandmother's permission gratified her vanity. But there was such a void at her table, among her dance partners, that it hardly mattered who was with her, since Horace was not.

After supper she returned to the ballroom, feeling weary, knowing that there were more hours to spend and wishing she could return home, wishing she were back in Yorkshire—no, not wishing that, for Lydia had benefited too much from her stay in Bath to wish that.

Suddenly, as she sat wondering exactly where she most wished to be, she was interrupted by her grandmother's greeting to Horace Crewe, his own deep voice, his eyes on her, his invitation to dance, his hand raised to take hers.

She floated off with him, looking at him as though in a dream, and when she got to the floor, discovered as he put his arm around her waist that this was yet another waltz. She would have said something in a laughing way, but the laughter had gone from their dealings together, and she blushed and clutched at his arms as though to steady herself against the terror of falling.

"I have timed my invitation ill, I see," he finally said after she had tripped over his feet a number of times.

"I am sorry," Anna almost sobbed, but swallowed hard against humiliation. "I still have not learned this dance."

"Perhaps some air, a walk in the garden. I am told they have a lovely statuary garden and a pleasant gazebo on a lake. Perhaps you would like to see it."

Anna nodded, failing to meet his eyes, and allowed him to escort her onto the grand balcony behind the dance floor, down a wide colonnaded staircase, onto a graveled walk.

Amid the couples who ambled along the walks, the footmen who circulated with trays of refreshments, and the older men and women taking the air were the silent, unmoving figures of Grecian statues. Draped in ancient gowns not unlike those of the living women who moved among them, they added a ghostly presence. The pearly night, brightened eerily by flambeaux, made the statues gleam and the water before them shimmer.

Anna held Crewe's arm and felt the texture of his coat. Occasionally his leg would brush against her skirt. He said nothing. And she was as silent.

Before them rose the gazebo, a temple with a domed

roof and an open wall of columns. It was encircled by wide steps, which they slowly climbed until they stood within the untenanted structure and gazed upon the waters gleaming before them.

Suddenly she felt his hands lift to her, one behind her neck, the other in the small of her back, and she was being tilted backward, her head tipped up. Her mouth came up, and his mouth was on hers. She raised her arms and wrapped them about his neck, pulling him down to her, opening her mouth to him.

"Horace," she moaned.

"Anna." Drawing back and looking at her, he gently lifted his hand and drew his knuckles against the top of her breasts above her gown. Then he brought his hand to her neck, her throat, and raised it to her lips. She kissed the back of his hand and watched him in pain and desire.

He bent his head, and they kissed again. This time his arms enfolded her as hers were wound around him. They stood pressed together as though they were a living statue, until they separated and caressed each other's faces with their hands, and read each other's mouths with their fingertips, smelled each other's flesh, and closed their eyes against the feel of the other's body.

Finally he pushed her slightly from him, holding her hands in his own.

"Anna. You are the most difficult female. What am I to do with you?"

Anna recoiled.

"You are a witch. You have caused me to crash, robbed me—wherever you go, trouble follows. But worse, you have ensnared me by every wile known to woman."

Anna drew back, pulling her hands from his. She could not endure this sparring. She was much too vulnerable, made so by his kisses and the knowledge of her love for him. She could not be sure whether he was kissing her because he loved her or was simply indulging himself with a woman he found attractive, could not be certain whether he distrusted her or merely pretended to. She knew that he had once been on the brink of offering for her. The change in his attitude caused her to lift eyes that were enormous and sad.

"Anna, are you going to talk to me?"

"I have nothing to say."

"Nothing to say? Come now," he said, chucking her under the chin.

"Stop it!" she cried at him. "Why are you treating me like this?"

"I think that should be obvious."

"You think I stole the ruby?"

Horace did not answer. He looked out over the water while she studied him.

"You do," she said quietly.

He turned back to her. "I really think, my dear, that I am so enamored of you that I do not care whether you did or not."

"You think me a thief."

"I did not say that, I said I do not care."

"How generous of you. Am I supposed to be grateful for that?"

"No, not grateful. You asked me what I thought—you should then be prepared to face what I think."

"Do you know what I think, my lord? I think that you are an insufferably vain and selfish man who thinks only of his own pleasure and does not care a whit for other people or their feelings."

"You being all other people, I assume, my dear Lady Anna?" He stepped away from her and leaned against one of the columns, regarding the spectacle of her anger with enjoyment.

"Ever since I met you, you have teased me, and . . . and . . ."

"Kissed you . . ."

Anna took two quick steps forward and slapped him soundly across the face.

"Ah," he said, rubbing his jaw. "The true Lady Anna shows herself. I have wondered where the famed Farrant temper had been hiding all this time."

"What Farrant temper?"

"Surely you know about your cousin Burleigh and his famous brawls."

"Oh, Burleigh," she said, turning away, uninterested.

"And your father, toper that he was, probably landed a few punches in his day."

"Leave my father out of this."

"Your father was a drunk, was he not?"

Anna lifted her hand to slap him again, but he was prepared and caught her wrist, and they stared at each other as he forced her straining arm to her side.

"Was he not?"

"My father was a dear and wonderful man who could not survive the death of my mother. He did turn to drink, yes. But he was not the kind of person you think he was. He was sad and lonely and . . . I am not to going to talk to you about him."

"And he killed himself."

"Be quiet!"

"Did he not kill himself? Perhaps I have been misinformed."

"You are cruel and hateful. I hate you."

"That is abundantly clear. Will hating me change your family's history? Will it make you any less inappropriate for a man in my position to marry?"

"Marry? Marry! Do you think I would consider marrying you even for a moment? I will tell you, Lord Crewe, I would not marry you if you were the last man on earth."

"And a traitor. I have not mentioned that your father was a traitor. But then, this is new information—I have only just learned it this evening."

Anna grew very still.

"You did not know this?" he asked.

She did not speak.

"Perhaps it is idle rumor."

"Who told you this?"

It was his turn to be silent.

"It would have to be Burleigh. He is the only one who knows."

"It was Burleigh."

"What did he tell you?"

"That your father sold the plans of the Sea Fencibles, and that when he was caught he killed himself."

Anna pressed her head against a cool marble column and closed her eyes.

Horace came to her, put a hand on her arm, and bent to kiss her neck.

She jerked away and looked at him with loathing. "I do not know why Burleigh told you. Yes, it is the truth. My father was a traitor. I am a thief. But I am not a whore, my lord."

She left him and proceeded down the wide marble stairs of the gazebo.

"Wait; you may as well return with me so that to our fellow guests we will seem to have been on a friendly stroll. Tell me, Anna, who told you about your father?"

"It is none of your business, my lord," she said coldly.

"I know it is not, my dear Lady Anna. But I want to know. Humor me."

She glanced at him briefly, giving him a glimpse of the distaste on her face.

"All right, do not humor me," he said with a glint of humor. His face grew suddenly very serious. "Anna, tell me, who told you?"

She shrugged. "Who would tell me, who would have known? Burleigh, of course. He was very kind—kept it quiet, allowed us to live quietly without having to be troubled by public gossip, by creditors—what difference can it make? Nothing matters."

"You are much too young to think that."

"And you, my lord, are too despicable a human being to know anything about the human heart. You will leave me, please."

The baron tagged along behind her up the stairs to the ballroom, and, after looking after her for a long moment, drew his heels together, bowed, and walked away.

Anna complained to her grandmother of a violent headache and begged to be allowed to return home. Lady Tretham was not overly concerned, for she was fatigued herself and not at all reluctant to leave, although it was not yet one o'clock.

Anna could not sleep that night. She tossed and turned until she finally threw off the bedclothes and went to the open window. Inhaling the fresh dawn air, she wondered how she could have ever thought she loved Lord Crewe. She knew now that she hated him. But why then did she feel so desolate?

Chapter
Fifteen

THE COUNTESS OF Tretham made a rare appearance at
the breakfast table the next morning. Anna could only push
her food about listlessly, but Lydia made up for her by
eating ravenously, begging Anna for her kipper if she was
not going to eat it, for her toast if she did not want it. The
women tacitly ignored her display of appetite, so delighted
were they to see it.

Not so Burleigh. "Lydia, have you not been taught that it
is impolite to eat from others' plates? Lydia, do not hunch
over your plate like that. Hold your head up and lift the
food to your mouth. It is shocking that your manners are
so reprehensible!"

Miss Bennet ate on in firm silence, and Lydia, who had
disliked Burleigh from the first and avoided him when she
could, glanced at Anna for help. When her sister winked,
Lydia endeavored to ignore him, although she did make
an effort to slow her eating, if only to save Miss Bennet's
reputation.

The countess occupied herself with the post, and Anna wondered why she had bothered to join them since she had not spoken one word to any of them. But when Anna was rising to go to her chamber to prepare for her ride with Caroline Wilcox, her grandmother stopped her.

"Anna, if I might have a word with you."

Anna smiled agreement but steeled herself.

They made their way to the morning room, bright with yellow chintz, and the countess directed the maid to bring coffee and tea to them there. When they were settled, she spoke.

"Do you know what is troubling Burleigh?"

"Burleigh?"

"Do not evade me, girl. Burleigh."

"Well . . ."

"Well . . ."

"Perhaps it is . . ." Anna was uncertain whether she should tell her grandmother of Burleigh's offer. Perhaps she would think she should have accepted him. But she never would. Odd, once she had told Horace Crewe that she would have done anything for Lydia. That was not true. She would not marry Burleigh.

"Have you forgotten my question, girl? Have your wits gone wandering?"

"No, Grandmother. Burleigh offered for me yesterday, and I refused him."

"Ah!" Lady Tretham raised her eyebrows and studied Anna, pursing her lips consideringly. "Why were you reluctant to tell me?"

"Because I thought you might wish me to marry him."

"What difference would it make to me whom you married?"

Anna heard only painful lack of interest in her grandmother's question, not aware that there might be any other interpretation. She answered her curtly. "None at all."

The countess took a sip of tea, aware that if it was not

Burleigh, something else, then, was causing her grand-daughter's spirits to sink. It could only be the ruby. She smiled to herself and spoke.

"So this is the famous daughter of the famous Louisa. One whiff of accusation, and she crumples like a rag doll."

Anna stiffened and turned to her with offended eyes. "I am doing nothing of the kind, madam."

"Oh, you have been a mooning, puny thing ever since yesterday. You had nothing to say for yourself coming back in the carriage last night after running from a ball with a 'headache.' You ate scarcely any breakfast. I am surprised that you would behave like this. You either took it and you should be glad you got away with it—after all, no one will find it now—or you did not and you should be outraged and clamoring for justice."

"Oh, Grandmother," Anna said wearily, "I did not take it. You must try to recover it, you must not give up on it. It is too beautiful. But do not look to me, for that will keep you from discovering who did take it."

"Do not worry, Anna, I have no intention of giving up on it. Let us not speak of it now. I want to talk about your plans. What do you wish to do now that you are in Bath? Besides wearing gowns of every shade of red you can find—have you any other goals?"

Anna drew herself up. "I do not think I am quite the silly thing you paint me, Grandmother. I am here because of Lydie, and my purpose is to see her recover."

"And then what?"

"What do you mean?"

"It seems to me she is well on her way to recovering—she is very happy, eating well, growing stronger—her full recovery is only weeks away. Then what?"

"Well . . ."

"Do you mean to stay here sponging off your elderly grandmother forever?"

Anna sighed. Burleigh was right, her grandmother was

finding her a financial burden. She would have to think about moving. "I realize I have spent a lot of money, Grandmother. If there were a way to repay you . . ."

"Do you intend for you and Lydie to live here indefinitely?"

"I have not thought very far ahead, it is true. I had thought of staying until she recovered and then returning to Yorkshire, but . . ."

"But?"

Anna smiled weakly, "I do not think I want to return to Yorkshire."

"Well, I agree with you there."

Anna shrugged.

Lady Tretham maintained a judicious silence.

"Grandmother, please, it would do me so much good to hear you say it would be all right to remain with you for a while without having to worry about the future. Through the summer, perhaps. If I could just not have to make any plans until, say, September."

"Anna, you really are the most difficult girl. . . ."

Anna wondered why everyone found her difficult. How difficult was she?

". . . I have waited for you to tell me that you wish to stay. To ask me if you might stay. You never give me a chance to show my generosity to you, my dear."

"Could you not just ask me? Must I beg?"

The countess mulled that over. "Touché, my dear. We are too alike—we neither want to beg. I want you here, my dear, and Lydie. You are like gifts to me. I am glad you had the courage to come. However . . ."

"Yes?"

"Well, nothing, now. Let that suffice. Is that acceptable, my dear?"

"Yes, Grandmother, and thank you." Anna rose and kissed her grandmother's cheek and retired to her room.

When she had donned the plum habit and popped in to

show herself to Lydia, she found that her younger sister was enduring the first dressing-down she had ever heard Miss Bennet administer to her.

"You must try to be attentive, Lydia. You have not only not prepared the translation, but you are not listening to me now."

"I am, I am, Benny, honestly I . . . Oh, Annie!"

Anna twirled around and left quickly, smiling apologetically to Miss Bennet for her added distraction.

Caroline's groom was holding their mounts in the road, and Anna almost forgot to greet her friend, so eager was she to inspect the first horse she had been allowed to ride in more than six years.

"Oh, but she is beautiful!"

"Do you like her?" Caroline asked, devouring every detail of Anna's riding habit. "She was my sister's, the one who was married last autumn."

"How could she bear to part with her?" Anna asked, patting the red roan's neck and admiring its beautiful coat.

"She married a vicar who cannot afford to keep her in horses."

"Did she? My grandfather was a vicar."

"An earl of Tretham?"

"No, my mother's father."

"Oh." Caroline cast an assessing glance at Anna, who, she could see, would surprise her often.

The young women mounted and, with a groom maintaining a decorous distance behind, proceeded sedately out of Bath to Charlcombe in the hills overlooking the city. Anna felt a burst of exhilaration. She laughed at Caroline, who laughed and nodded, and together they urged their horses forward and broke into a canter, which in a few moments they released into a full gallop.

They swept through a high field and into woods that slowed their speed. They came to a chill beck running slowly in the height of summer, and they loosened the reins to allow their mounts to drink. Returning to the fields, they again let the horses have their heads and romped through a succession of high fields, then circled back and came upon a farmhouse where a child of no more than three stood soberly sucking its thumb and watching them.

Anna asked if they could have a cup of milk and tossed the child a coin. The child—whether a girl or boy was not clear given the long skirts and full curls of infancy—brought out two tin cups of fresh sweet milk, and the women drank their fill. Wiping her mouth with the back of her hand, Anna handed her cup back to the child, and she and Caroline began the leisurely return to Bath, riding slowly enough to allow conversation.

Anna wished she could speak openly to Caroline. She would have welcomed the chance to unburden her heart about Burleigh, the missing ruby, her grandmother—and Horace Crewe. But instead she found pleasure in Caroline's intelligent comments about Bath, mutual acquaintances, and books they had read.

The hours had passed swiftly, and Anna was soon back at the Royal Crescent, happier and more at peace with herself than she had been earlier. The house was quiet. Lydia was napping, the countess was closeted with an old friend, and Miss Bennet was at the shops on a commission from Anna—tracking the exact shade of pearly lavender she desired for an evening gown.

Anna decided to wash her hair before the evening's concert. Afterward, as she sat before a gentle fire, tossing her hair from side to side and combing it out with her fingers, she felt the quiet of the house around her. She went to the window and watched the carriages passing the sloping lawn in front of the Crescent.

She returned to the fire and succumbed to the stillness, to the drowsiness the bath had induced, and lay down on her bed on her stomach, her warm, damp hair spread over her like a coverlet, and fell asleep.

After tea, Anna, Lydia, and the countess set out to attend a concert at the Assembly Rooms. It was the first time that Lydia had attended a formal engagement, and Anna enjoyed helping her prepare for it. She had chosen a pale yellow muslin gown embroidered in deep gold, and with her wild golden curls she looked like a burnished angel. At least, so Anna thought.

When they took their seats in the crowded room, it was obvious that others thought so, too. Lydia found the company enthralling and asked Anna questions about every interesting person she saw, which by Anna's count amounted to just about everyone.

Two men, however, did not share the audience's interest in the lovely sisters. One was Burleigh. He had gone to the concert separately and lounged against the wall ignoring them pointedly. The man he was talking to, however, whom Anna thought looked feral and dissipated, continually threw glances their way, persuading her that Burleigh must be talking about her, even though he might try to seem oblivious.

The other man who was not paying them any attention was Horace Crewe. He was standing next to a row of chairs at the end of which sat the dark-eyed beauty Anna had seen him dancing with the previous night. Anna kept her eyes from him as much as she could and found some distraction in Lydia's excitement.

At the intermission George Ives appeared from the back of the room and claimed Lydia's attention. From the high color and obliviousness to the rest of the world they both exhibited, Anna was sure that whatever George felt for Lydia was reciprocated. She felt a stab of envy that these two young people should so easily find love, a love with no complications that time itself would not resolve.

She was hailed by Caroline, and together they left the room to seek refreshments. As they moved among the strolling guests, Horace Crewe approached. Anna felt like a young girl, afraid he would notice her, afraid he would not.

He glanced in their direction, nodding curtly toward Caroline. Anna felt sick. Caroline was surprised. He and Anna had set tongues wagging only a few nights earlier when they had danced together, and now they did not even acknowledge each other. Caroline would have loved to ask, but Anna's high color and determined chatter gave her to understand she was trying to avoid that very possibility.

The next day Anna and Caroline went riding again. Caroline insisted that Anna have the use of the roan mare so that she could ride even when Caroline was not able to. This sign of friendship deeply touched Anna. They spent the rest of the morning in Lady Tretham's library, where they found an Italian grammar and tried to translate lines from an Italian song they had heard at the concert.

That evening the countess, Burleigh, and Anna attended a small card party at Lady Sally Evans'. Anna wore her most modest gown, a slim sheath of deep purple satin with a high neck, which did not strike the men who admired it as particularly demure.

She had not advanced more than two feet into the crowded drawing room when she saw Horace Crewe leaning toward a plain, brown-haired woman whose serious demeanor in the face of Horace's quite clearly flirtatious and bantering conversation puzzled her. She looked quickly away before he could notice her and kept her head determinedly facing away from that quarter of the room.

Unluckily, when the tables were made up for commerce, Anna found herself seated at a large table with him and the young woman, as well as with Burleigh, among others who were strangers to her. It was easy for her to remain quiet among so many. It was also easy for her to overhear Horace's conversation with the young woman, whom the neighbor on Anna's left had referred to as one of the richest young women on the marriage mart.

Under other circumstances, Anna would have found their conversation amusing, but she found a perverse pleasure in realizing that Horace was fighting an uphill battle in the conversation. The woman was stiff, rarely deviating from the formulas of polite conversation. When she was not responding with a "Yes, I see" or a "Goodness" or a "No, indeed," what conversation she initiated seemed exclusively to concern her older brother, a worthy named Robert, and his excellence as a player of whist.

Anna eavesdropped with what she hoped was convincing indifference, feeling offended that he would prefer this woman's insipid conversation to her own and trying not to feel devastated by that fact.

She was startled to realize that Burleigh had been addressing her.

"Would you attend, Anna?"

"I am sorry, Burleigh. What did you say?"

"I must remind you that this is not a family card game. You really must not cheat as you do at home."

Anna, who had never played a game of cards with Burleigh in her life, stared at him openmouthed. Then, collecting herself, she looked at her cards and realized she had five. She blushed and tried to figure out what to do with the extra two when Burleigh threw down his cards and pushed his stakes toward the middle of the table saying, "Perhaps we should deal another hand."

Anna, still flushed, took in a few of the slightly frowning faces and decided to flee the situation altogether.

"I am so sorry, I really was not attending," she said as she pushed back her chair. "I have never been good at cards. Please forgive me."

As she turned to leave the table, she let her gaze pass over Horace Crewe, who seemed to be lost in contemplation of the jeweled buttons on Burleigh's waistcoat. She was glad he had not faced her in her shame.

Fortunately the party broke up early, and Anna sought refuge in Lydia's room when she returned home. It was a balm to sit quietly before the fire with Lydia and Miss Bennet.

Lydia sat cross-legged on the floor, tangled in a maze of embroidery silks she was trying to separate. She was in the middle of stitching a picture of a bowl of flowers, an undertaking urged on her by her friend Meggy. Although Lydia devoutly admired Meggy and was determined to become an accomplished needlewoman, she detested it.

"With just the simplest turn of your fingers, you can get the thread all twisted. And mine is always so dirty. I do not know why, but even if I have just washed my hands, the minute I pull the pale yellow silk through, it is dingy gray. Not only that, but when I chose this yellow, it seemed to be just the color, but look at it, it turns green next to the pink, but look at Meggy's, see how well she did hers? Oh, I wish I could do as well."

Anna laughed. "And this is supposed to be something to give you pleasure, Lydie?"

Lydia pulled a face. "It really does not, but if I keep trying, surely I shall improve."

Miss Bennet said, "You know, when I was young, the fashion was for making pictures by using the dried petals of flowers, cutting them into shapes and pressing them so that they formed a picture of a garden or landscape."

Lydia looked up with interest. "That sounds like something I could do."

"Well, not until you make a good showing of those silks you have bought, young woman."

"Oh, Benny, we need not be so pinchpenny now," said Anna. "Surely we do not need to require her to finish this project because of a few shillings' worth of silks."

Miss Bennet looked reprovingly at Anna, and Anna reminded herself that if they were to leave her grandmother's for another household founded on genteel poverty, such economies would be needed again.

To mollify Miss Bennet and her own conscience—usually the same thing—she added, "We shall save them. We will use them to embroider Lydie's trousseau."

Lydia blushed, and they continued chattering and nibbling on the little cakes that Cook had smuggled up to Lydia, hidden among what looked at first glance to be a very plain tea.

Suddenly into the cozy room, without even the forewarning of a knock, came Herndon, Lady Tretham's maid.

"Lady Anna, I do not know what to do, but I cannot find Her Ladyship's sapphire diadem."

Chapter
Sixteen

ANNA GREW WHITE. She rose, trembling, unable to speak, and stared at Herndon.

Miss Bennet asked, "My good woman, what are you saying?"

"Her Ladyship's diadem, the Tudor one. The one with the big sapphire and the old-style uncut diamonds, the round diamonds. You must know of it, the Tretham diadem? It's priceless and it's missing."

"How do you know it is missing?" Miss Bennet persisted.

"After the loss of the ruby," she said with a slanting look at Anna, "we decided to inventory all my lady's jewels. While she was at the card party this afternoon, I began— and it is missing."

"Where was it kept?"

"In a coffer of its own. The original coffer, as old as the diadem. It's so beautiful . . ."

Miss Bennet turned to Anna, who had been too stunned to follow the conversation. She did, however, make a slight gesture toward Lydia to indicate she should be spared this, and, looking at her sister, Anna reminded herself that she must gather her forces together to endure this.

"I shall come with you and help you look for it before Grandmother returns so that she need not worry about it."

Miss Herndon began to protest but found herself being escorted out before she could say another word.

The nightmare unfolded slowly, from a search of Lady Tretham's room through the questioning of the servants. Anna braced for the countess' return with the small hope that perhaps she had herself decided to store it in a new place. But when she did return, Anna had to face the fact that she had not and, witnessing her grandmother's ashen anxiety and sudden confusion about where it might be, could only try to comfort her with watered wine.

Burleigh, who had arrived with her, was apoplectic, and Anna had to endure a burgeoning sense of dread that became almost unendurable once she had been able to retreat to her own chamber. The next day, in the face of Lady Tretham's continuing confusion, Burleigh directed a search of the mansion from the cellars to the servants' rooms in the attics.

In late morning the diadem was found wrapped in a shawl of Anna's and stuffed under the mattress of her bed.

Anna was not surprised. She had felt the dread inevitability of her guilt.

Her grandmother did not call for her at once. Rather she had to wait through the midday meal, which she took with Lydia and Meggy, who were subdued without knowing the reason for Anna's low spirits and the household uproar. The hours dragged on, full of imaginings of trials and gaol, of disgrace and abandonment. Finally the summons came.

She descended on weak knees and entered the doors of the room where she had made her first entrance to her grandmother's life. The countess and Burleigh sat exactly as they had on that first day.

She approached them exactly as a prisoner would approach the bench and realized that there was no chair set for her, that she was expected to stand through what would be a stern interrogation.

Burleigh began. "Since you have arrived at my grandmother's home, unannounced and unexpected, there have been two major thefts of her most valuable jewels. In addition, you have bled her dry with your extravagant purchases . . ."

"Burleigh, allow me to speak for myself. It is clear, my dear, that there is something terrible afoot in this house. It is clear that either you are involved in the thefts or made to look as though you are. Either way, it is a frightfully serious matter."

"Grandmother, please allow me to explain."

"Anna, I do not need an explanation from you. If you need money, for whatever purpose, for debts, gambling, blackmail, whatever the reason, I will give it to you gladly. You need not take my jewels. If you have not taken them, then I must offer you my protection. Whichever is true, you are welcome in my home."

Burleigh lowered his brows and glowered at Anna, as if defying her to believe in her grandmother's generosity. Anna found Lady Tretham's tolerance of her possible guilt as hard to bear as Burleigh's enmity. She said nothing, for she was determining in her mind that she would have to leave—even if it required asking her grandmother to help her establish another residence—she must leave.

Burleigh interrupted her thoughts. "Are you not going to thank your grandmother, Anna?"

"Of course. Thank you, Grandmother."

"There is something else," Burleigh said. "I think you should go away, Anna, until the scandal of this theft has been hushed up. Your going out now into the society of Bath would be painful for your grandmother and me, although it is our grandmother we must most consider. If we are not important enough to you, there is Lydia—I am sure you would not wish to destroy her chances for acceptance by becoming the cynosure of Bath."

"But there is no scandal, Burleigh," she protested. "Who else knows of this?"

"When I was at the Pump Room this afternoon, when I stopped at Kaline's, the jeweler . . . indeed, Anna, everywhere I went I was greeted with questions about you and the theft. Everyone is wondering how my grandmother can countenance your presence. Of course it is known."

"But how?" Anna felt sick.

Burleigh shrugged. "Servants, I suppose."

"Oh." Anna foresaw the house becoming a prison to her as Yorkshire had been. Whereas poverty had once kept her secluded, now it would be this ghastly suspicion, which in her heart she knew, although unjustified in regard to her grandmother's jewels, was amply justified in relation to a certain diamond stickpin.

"That is all nonsense," the countess interrupted forcefully. "Anna is not going to hide away as though the rumors are true. Anyone in the house might have hidden the crown in her chamber. Craig—I have had him only a year. Even if you had employed him before that, Burleigh, neither of us knows much about him. And Herndon became my dresser only two years ago. Perhaps I should not have trusted her with so much responsibility."

"But she discovered the theft!" Burleigh interjected.

"*That* theft, Burleigh, but the ruby is still missing. Perhaps this is a ruse to point suspicion at Anna and to take our attention from the missing ruby. As long as there is doubt about who stole what, Anna, my granddaughter, will carry out her normal social duties, including the ball tonight."

"Oh, Grandmother, I could not. Please, allow me to remain here."

"Anna, you will go to the ball with me, and you will go with your head held high. Do you understand?"

Anna studied the determination in her grandmother's eyes and nodded.

That night she walked into the Upper Rooms wearing a rose-violet satin gown with an overdress of diaphanous ruby, wishing, again, that she had one gown of modest design she could have hidden behind. Her grandmother took her arm as they stood in the drafty vestibule and prodded her forward. Although a few people nodded at her grandmother, no one addressed a word to her.

But she was not ignored. She felt all eyes on her, from her hair, crowned with a circlet of roses, to her toes, clad in silver slippers. She sensed the stir she caused although she did not have the courage to bring her focus in from the distant point at which it was fixed to discern individual faces.

It was as though people parted to make way for them, careful not to be touched even by the hem of her gown as they made their way through the throng into the largest of the rooms. She felt as though people broke off their conversations and forgot to resume them.

The Countess of Tretham stopped before two chairs in the very center of the longest line of chairs along the far wall, beyond the archway to the card room, and sat down with great ceremony. Anna would rather have run desperately out into the cool evening, or at best, kept walking so as to work off her nervousness and not offer herself up as a sitting target for curious stares and speculative gossip.

Burleigh was present, Anna noticed, seemingly immersed in conversation himself, neither noticing them nor coming to relieve them of their isolation. No men solicited Anna as a dance partner. No women stopped to talk to her or her grandmother. After about twenty minutes spent in awkward silence, to her great relief she saw Caroline Wilcox approach and she rose with a smile of welcome, holding out her hand. But Caroline noticed her and, flushed and embarrassed, turned away.

Anna stood as still as stone, watching Caroline's retreating back. The horror was now driven home. She resumed her seat, oblivious to everything but the ferocious desire to cry and the ferocious need not to do so before all these people who were now only enemies.

Neither she nor her grandmother spoke. Her grandmother stared straight ahead, seemingly unaware of Anna's misery. She inclined her head occasionally to the handful of those who were willing or curious enough to venture a nod before looking quickly elsewhere. For a moment Anna tried to follow suit, but her gaze fell to the floor, despite her best intentions.

It was with complete shock, then, that she heard a voice address them. It was a greater shock when it pierced her consciousness that it was Lord Crewe standing before them. He was asking her to dance, a pleasant expression on his face, as though this were the most ordinary moment at the most ordinary ball in the world.

It took her a moment to gather herself together to respond. "I do not wish to dance, Lord Crewe, thank you."

"I did not expect that you would, Lady Anna, but please, do me the honor."

"No."

"Anna, don't be a goose. Of course she will dance with you, Horace."

"Thank you, madam," Horace said with a twinkle in his eye.

"Very well, if I must." Anna rose and took Crewe's outstretched hand.

When they had joined the dance, the baron said, "Are you not going to thank me for coming to your rescue?"

"I did not need to be rescued."

"You were enjoying sitting there quite ostracized, scorned by everyone in Bath, with no prospects for the evening but to stare at the floor?"

"Yes."

Crewe laughed. Anna knew she sounded like a fool, but feeling the fool was not half so bad as giving him satisfaction.

"Since everyone in the Rooms seems to be watching you, my dear, why don't we struggle to give the impression that we are talking politely and having a pleasant time?"

"Because we are not."

"How pleasant the room is at this time of the year, is it not, with all the masses of flowers they can use for its decorating?"

"Please return me to my grandmother. I find this intolerable."

"And look at all the lovely flowers in the ladies' hair. Your own roses are a triumph! I prefer them to the anemones you wore the other evening. Anemones wilt too soon."

"Please release me, I am warning you, or I shall cause a scene."

"And doesn't the orchestra play divinely, my dear Lady Anna?"

Anna slipped from his arm and began to walk away. But Crewe sprang after her and intercepted her as though she were only executing some rather more exotic steps in the dance and guided her back to their place in the set.

"And how lovely you yourself look. You really do have the most remarkable sense of color, Lady Anna. You resemble a rainbow, or a swaying fuchsia on a summer breeze, or . . ."

"Very well, I will concede this much. I shall dance with you, but only on the condition that you do not utter one single word more."

"Ah, you do me such honor to dance with me while all of Bath looks upon you with censorious eyes."

"I am not grateful. I will not be grateful. If you choose to dance with me, it must be to inflict some form of punishment on us both."

"I believe I have inflicted quite enough punishment on you, my dear. Can you ever forgive me for my appalling conduct? It was wrong of me to be insensible to your feelings, to broach the business of your father's misfortune in such a callous way. Will you forgive me, Anna?"

"No."

"The voice of honesty. Smile, my little spider. You look as if you are being persecuted."

"I am!"

"No, you are not, you are being given the attention of one of the most eligible bachelors in all of England and part of Scotland as well. Now smile."

"I would rather take off all my clothes and dance the tarantella."

"If you prefer."

Anna laughed for the first time.

"That is better."

"I did not mean it."

"No, I am sure you did not," he said in a soothing tone.

"Ha! The dance is over!"

"Yes, and you only unbent once. Very good, my lady."

With that he bowed and left, and her hand was immediately sought by George Ives. She was touched and grateful for his attention, for although it was clear that he was determined to show his loyalty to her—and to Lydia—he was very self-conscious and embarrassed by the situation and showed it by talking constantly and staring fixedly at her.

She was almost relieved to be returned to her grandmother's side, but instead of being allowed to retreat into her shell again, Horace, who had been carrying on a quite public and determined conversation with the countess, claimed her for another dance.

When they had taken their places, he said, "Tell me about this latest theft of yours."

Chapter
Seventeen

"*I STOLE MY* grandmother's diadem—the Tretham sapphire-and-diamond crown that dates from the Tudors—and hid it under my mattress wrapped in one of my shawls."

"Not very imaginative of you."

"No, but then I am such a very starting-out kind of thief."

"Let us see, how much experience have you had?"

"Well, there is your stickpin, of course, and then the ruby, and now this. That is all really just getting going, you might say, although you do have to admire my taste."

"Where is the ruby?"

"Oh, I hid that in the toe of one of my dancing slippers."

"Not very clever."

"No? What would have been clever?"

"Oh, I suppose to have cut it down into smaller jewels and worn them openly while everyone hunted it, or to have tossed it to a beggar, something like that."

"I will consider your suggestions, my lord."

"Anna, you are very sad, for all your defiant talk."

She looked away, maintaining a frozen smile.

My God, she is beautiful, he thought. He gripped her hand tightly; she winced and looked quickly at him. They regarded each other for a moment.

Then he spoke. "A pity there is no gazebo at the Assembly Rooms."

"I have learned my lesson about quitting the dance floor, my lord."

"Anna, do you so regret our kisses?"

She paled.

"Forgive me, I will change the subject. What is this puppy love George has for your sister?"

It was the only subject he could have chosen that she could have spoken on with any pleasure. "Ah, I think they have fallen in love. She is so happy. He has even asked me if he might court her. I had to tell him she is only sixteen. He is what, nineteen?"

"Twenty, and an old friend, even if he is young."

"How do you know him?"

"He was my brother's friend."

"I did not know you had a brother."

"I do not, anymore. Clive died four years ago."

"I am sorry."

"My parents are dead as well, which is why, of course, I am the seventh Baron of Trent. I would rather have them than the title."

"You have no family left?"

"I have a sister who lives in Essex with her gentleman farmer husband. She seldom goes into society."

"She sounds pleasing."

"She is not at all pleasing—she is a tart-tongued harridan. But I am fond enough of her."

They separated in the dance. When they were rejoined, he asked, "Will you go riding with me? I have seen you out with Caroline Wilcox."

"I plan never to leave my grandmother's house again after tonight!"

"I had not thought you lacking in courage, Anna."

"That shows how little you know me. I intend to quit Bath as soon as I can, for Lydie's sake as well as my own. She cannot be asked to share my ostracism. We will find a place to live simply where she can enjoy country outings."

"A remote, bleak house under dripping trees in Yorkshire?"

"With my grandmother's help, perhaps not. But we will remain in the south. I will not remove her from a climate that has done her so much good."

"It is a shame you got to know Yorkshire when you were in such want, Lady Anna. It is beautiful—I have a hunting lodge there. Perhaps you . . . Ah, there is Burleigh bearing down on us looking like Jupiter."

Anna dropped his hand and turned to Burleigh.

"Your grandmother is quite unwell, Anna. It is time we left for home."

"Oh, no, I knew we should not have come. This has been too much for her. Where is she?"

"In the entry hall. She is faint. Your behavior has proved to be more than she could bear."

Anna hurried through the crowded room to find her grandmother leaning against a friend who was fanning her pale face and perspiration-beaded brow.

"Oh, Anna, thank heavens. Come, dear, give me your arm. I had no intention of leaving so soon, but I feel so unwell."

"Of course, Grandmother," Anna responded, bending to take her grandmother's elbow. It was not Burleigh who took the other, but Horace, who had followed Anna from the room without her knowledge.

They supported the countess between them to the carriage, which had already been called. Burleigh, hovering about uselessly, made as though to climb in after them, but Lady Tretham waved him away. "I want to talk to Anna, please. I shall talk with you tomorrow. There is something urgent she and I need to discuss."

"Of course," said Burleigh. Horace Crewe noted the look of self-satisfaction. As Burleigh stepped back, Crewe exchanged a glance with George Ives, and they nodded briefly to each other. After the carriage pulled away, they continued together, talking in low voices and, instead of returning to the Rooms, departed in separate directions.

Within the carriage the countess broke into harsh sobbing, which Anna was unable to stem despite her efforts to soothe and reassure her grandmother. They parted when they arrived back at the mansion—Anna forced to pace in agitation in her chamber.

When Anna was called for, she discovered her grandmother, attired in more comfortable clothes, resting in a chaise before the fire in her own bedchamber. The sight was distressing to Anna, who had come to think of her grandmother as invulnerable.

The countess waved her maids away, no longer weeping, but still very obviously distressed.

"I have just learned something, my dear, that has terribly distressed me. It is about your father."

Anna sank to the bed and looked at her hands in silence.

"Burleigh told me. He said I should know. That your father . . . that Edward was . . . a . . . a spy."

"I am sorry that he told you, Grandmother."

"Did you know?"

"Yes, but I do not care. I love him as much as I ever did."

"I think it will break my heart, Anna."

"There was no need for you to know."

"I suppose Burleigh believed he had to tell me."

"Burleigh's sense of duty frequently hurts others."

"What do you mean?"

"He told Horace Crewe as well."

The countess sat up straight. "Why?"

"I do not know. Perhaps he thought . . . perhaps he thought Horace should know the worst about me."

"Is Horace Crewe interested in you, beyond dancing with you many too many times, I mean?"

"I do not know. Well, I thought so at one time, but I think that now . . . I do not know." Anna blinked back tears.

"He would have made a wonderful husband for you. And he is very wealthy. And his beautiful home—Pitcombe Hall . . . Oh, Anna, I feel old."

"Oh, Grandmother!" Anna cried, leaning toward her and taking her hand. "It is all my fault. Coming here . . . bringing all this trouble down upon you."

"No, dear, I was an ostrich with my head in the sand. I knew nothing of all this. I have lived comfortably in Bath while you and Lydie suffered the consequences of my son's actions."

"You have more than made up for that by your welcome to us now. I only regret that my father's debts . . ."

"Debts? Yes, what is it, Herndon?"

"My lady, you must rest," Herndon said, coming into the room with a hot drink for the countess and a scowl for Anna.

Anna bent over and kissed her grandmother, bidding her to sleep well, glad to be allowed the peace of her own bedchamber at last.

As she slipped off her gown and braided her hair, she listened at the door and, deciding that Lydia was asleep, gave herself over to her thoughts.

One of them gave her strange comfort. She realized that in her grandmother's concern for her, in the countess' self-blame for her past neglect of Anna and Lydia, lay the seeds of forgiveness—even affection. It comforted her to know this. Tenderness and gratitude for her grandmother outweighed her earlier fears and her pride.

Her thoughts turned to Horace. What had he meant by his strange behavior at the Assembly Rooms? Was it possible that he was not going to be deterred by her father's actions or her own? Was it possible that his kindness was more than simple kindness, that it meant a revival of his interest in her, his desire for her?

She surrendered to the seductive images of him, of his face, his hair, the way his black hair sprang from his temples in thick waves, how much she had resisted touching it with her hands. She thought of his height, the strength in his thighs, his arms . . . She lay in the dark, blushing.

After a night of alternating disturbing dreams and sleeplessness, Anna awoke early and discovered that the comforting thoughts about her grandmother and her dreams of Horace had receded with the night. Her worries renewed with the day.

Who was the thief? Why was she being made to seem the thief? Would she ever be able to prove her innocence? To gain the respect of society?

Would Horace have danced with her if he considered her a thief? Perhaps he enjoyed dancing with someone under suspicion for a crime. It was the kind of thing that would amuse him, she knew.

And the stickpin. If he ever told anyone of the stickpin, her guilt would be confirmed in everyone's eyes. For his silence alone, she was in his thrall.

She flung off the covers, threw on her riding habit, and was out on Caroline's mare—daring to avail herself of Caroline's invitation, despite yesterday's snubbing—before the kitchen maids had rubbed the sleep from their eyes.

As she rode through the now familiar hills, she allowed herself to think about Caroline's snub last night. That had hurt as much as anything. How could her friendship, which had shown itself in the loan of this beautiful horse, be so completely shattered by rumor? Caroline had not even taken the trouble to ask her about the rumors.

She rode alone, defying convention, and made for the same beck she and Caroline had found and returned to in their rides together. She did not see the small child. She was not in the mood to stop at the little stream, but instead rode over the fields with pounding speed and then circled back again, returning home by another route. By the time she returned to the Crescent, hot and weary, she hoped she would be able to nap.

But the house was in turmoil.

Lydia was missing.

After questioning the excited, almost hysterical servants, Anna discovered that Lydia seemed to have gone out before breakfast. Shaking and terrified, she learned that Miss Bennet had been dressing in her own chamber, Nurse Brookens had been talking with Cook, and none of the maids had seen her leave. The footman at the front door had helped her into a carriage he had not recognized, which Lydia had told him Meggy's family had sent for her.

A footman returned with Meggy's father, who told them that they had not sent any carriage around, that Meggy had no idea where Lydia might be, had not seen her since the day before, and had no plans with her.

Lady Tretham remained in bed, still shaken by the discovery of the night before, and had to be told. It fell to Anna to do so, and conquering her own terror, she did, only to watch her grandmother grow frail before her eyes. She appeared dazed and unable to focus, and it was Anna who summoned Burleigh and asked him to gather friends to ride to inns, posting houses, as well as places in Bath where Lydia might have gone on a whim.

But she could not imagine any whim that would take Lydia away in a carriage without first telling her about it.

Anna thought of asking for the assistance of Horace and George Ives, but until she knew whether or not Lydia was involved in a foolish but safe undertaking, she was reluctant to do so. If George were to think Lydia, like Anna herself, badly governed, impulsive, or reckless, might he not break off his connection with her? She had to protect Lydia.

Finally, having dispatched as many people on as many errands as she could think of, she went to her chamber, and there, in the wardrobe, found a note. As hot as she was, Anna grew chill at the sight of it. It was addressed to Anna, but it was not in Lydia's hand.

Anna sat stiffly on the bed and read. " 'We have Lady Lydia. If you want her alive, you must bring the Farrant snuffbox collection to the stream where you usually ride. If you do as you are told, she will be released unharmed. But if you tell anyone, or fail to appear by noon with what we demand, you will never see her again. Destroy this.' "

Noon! It was only a little more than an hour until noon! How could she possibly do everything the note said? Where was Lydia? Was she safe?

Oh, God, she had to be safe. She could not be ill . . . hurt . . .

Anna thought she was going to be sick, but struggled to her feet and forced herself to think calmly.

Should she tell Burleigh? Her grandmother? She did not dare. Anna spun around the room, moving distractedly from one object to another, trying to put her thoughts in order, undoing the top buttons of her habit only to button them again, reading the note only to crumple it and then smooth it and read it again.

How could they take Lydie? Didn't they know she was ill? She could not possibly withstand harsh treatment. *Oh, God, please let her be safe.*

Anna fought the sobs that threatened to break from her and crashed her fists down on her dressing table and cursed. She had no time to cry—she must ride to the meeting place.

What snuffbox collection? Where was it? She vaguely remembered some small boxes, jeweled, enameled, that rested in a cabinet in the parlor. Would these be what was meant? Were they valuable? Would the cabinet be locked?

There was nothing to do but exactly what the note commanded. She read it once more and hurled it into the fire, watching it burn, her face becoming hard.

She slipped downstairs carrying a paisley shawl that she hoped would be ample enough to hold the boxes. As she went through the hallway, a footman, polishing the looking glass, nodded to her. She nodded back as calmly as she could and let herself into the parlor.

It was empty. The cabinet was on her left, opposite the fireplace, between the tall windows that overlooked the lawn before the Crescent. She closed the door gently and made her way to the cabinet.

It was a new piece of furniture, graceful and simple, and she realized from its shallow shelves and general design that it must have been built to house the collection. The double glass doors were closed, both keyholes empty. Anna tried to pry them open with her fingernails but the doors did not budge.

She was very hot. She had not realized how tense she was.

The key. Craig might have it. She could not ask him. Perhaps it was in one of the drawers beneath the shelves . . . She bent to pull the top drawer out—it was filled with an assortment of globes, candles, and an old snuffer.

The second drawer was empty except for what looked like a forgotten damask table covering. She shook it out, but no key fell from its folds.

The bottom drawer held only a small metal box tucked over to the side. With shaking fingers, Anna picked it up and heard something shift inside as she did so.

Just then the door to the hall began to swing open, and Anna had time only to press the drawer closed and move to a window embrasure before Craig walked in.

As coolly as she could, she spoke to him. "Has there been any word of my sister?"

"No, I'm afraid not, my lady."

"I have been wondering," she said, turning toward the window again, as though she had been there only to watch for Lydia, "has anyone gone to the stables where her colt is kept?"

"No, my lady, I do not believe so. I will direct a footman to do so immediately."

He bowed himself out of the room.

Instantly Anna opened the box and discovered a key. She hurried to the cabinet, inserted it, turned it gently, and the snuffboxes were immediately in her hand. She dropped them hurriedly into her looped-up shawl, opened the other door, removed those boxes as well, returned the metal box to the drawer, and closed the doors. Slipping the key into the shawl, she knotted it together as tightly as she could, to keep them all from clanking.

She pressed the bundle under her arm, crossed to the door, and opened it slightly. The footman was in the rear of the hall, speaking to a maid. He saw Anna and gestured to her that he would come immediately to let her out, but she shook her head and slipped out the front door.

Her walk to the Wilcoxes' was the longest of her life. Never, not even in her most daring red gown, had she felt so conspicuous.

She shifted from foot to foot while the groom saddled the mare, ignoring his look of surprise and disapproval that the weary mare should be taken out so soon after being so hard ridden.

Chapter
Eighteen

ONCE SHE WAS away from the stable, Anna looped the shawl over the pommel, braced her leg against it, and took off at a sedate trot until free of the city. Once beyond its precincts she urged the horse into the fastest gallop it could attain.

As she flew over Charlcombe, past the farmhouse, it occurred to Anna for the first time that she might well be in danger. She shook her head, amazed that she had not thought of it before. But concern for Lydia and preoccupation with securing the ransom had kept her from thinking ahead to what would take place at the edge of the stream.

I should have brought a weapon, she thought. A knife. Or perhaps her grandmother still had her grandfather's pistols. Why had she not thought to arm herself?

But soon she was deep into the woods. She slowed the horse, then brought it to a halt while still within the trees. Peering between them, she could see no sign of anyone near the stream. She considered waiting within the shelter of the trees, but feared that if she did not show herself in time, harm would come to Lydia.

Breathing deeply to steady herself, she urged the horse forward, broke from the cover, and arrived at the bank of the narrow waterway. She was alone. Twisting about on the saddle, dancing with the horse in circles, she looked around, but no one appeared.

She listened, but all she could hear was the thudding of her own heart and the nickering of the horse. She watched the horse to see if it would give any sign of sensing the presence of others, but it was oblivious to everything but the cool, running water before it.

Anna waited, trying to determine what to do, and then started up the bank toward the north. She must have ridden for a mile or two before she swung the horse around and headed in the opposite direction, past her starting point, a mile, two miles, three miles.

She began to panic. She could not force the horse to move fast enough. The idea that she could miss the kidnappers, that they would harm Lydia, forced her to plunge in one direction and then another. It was her mount, lathered and harried, that persuaded Anna to stop. She slid from the saddle, tied the horse near the stream, and walked as aimlessly and frantically as she had ridden.

She guessed it must be well past noon but could not know for sure. Desperately she remounted the horse and made the circuit again, splashing through water where the trees grew too close to the bank to allow her to ride along it, wading through thick mud in the increasing heat of midday, slipping on the steep grassy slopes, and watching, watching for the smallest movement, listening for any sign of another human being.

In despair she returned to the grassy verge, slipped off the horse, and nearly fell to the ground, exhausted and without hope.

Lydia was not there.

That one fact was all she knew.

Anna lay back on her elbows, panting for breath, trying to consider possible courses of action, not giving in to the yearnings she felt for magical rescues or for regrets that they had ever come to Bath.

She jumped to her feet. She simply must have missed them. She hauled herself onto the horse and once more rode down the eastern bank of the river.

Not more than a couple hundred yards away, she heard what she had been listening for. The sound of hoofbeats, the noise of a horse crashing through underbrush.

She urged the mare to a small spinney and held it and herself rigid, praying not to be seen. It was a single rider, a man. She could see wide shoulders in a bottle green coat. The rider came into the clearing and looked around.

It was Horace Crewe.

Anna sucked in her breath, appalled. She nudged the horse deeper into the spinney and stared at him.

Horace Crewe! Abducting Lydia? Then his kindness at the ball had only been a way to deceive her—he must have been planning this for a long time. He had taken his revenge on her, after all, for the stickpin. A revenge of the cruelest sort.

Crewe hesitated at the bank, just as she had, his horse angled away from the river. Suddenly he dug his heels into the horse's flanks and took off as she had, no doubt to make a circuit of the riverbank.

She could not run away. For Lydia's sake she must face him. She dismounted and studied the bundle on the saddlehorn. She did not believe that he really wanted the treasure—one of the richest men in England? No, more likely, he had required the ransom only to trap her into another theft, one that Craig had probably discovered by now and raised an alarm about.

She reached up and freed the shawl with its jumbled treasure and tossed it behind a tree. There was no reason to give it over until she had to, once he proved he had Lydia.

A part of her felt very sick. Horace Crewe, abducting Lydie. How could he do it? What a day of terror her sister must have endured!

Too weary to think of anything else to do, Anna walked to the clearing and sat down to await Crewe's reappearance. It was like awaiting a sentence of death. No, no, she must not think that way, she was waiting for Lydie, for Lydie to be safe, to be with her again. She tried to feel hope, but could not.

Soon she heard the rustling of the undergrowth and the dull thud of hooves that heralded his return. She stood, and simultaneously he saw her and reined in abruptly.

For a long time he stared down at her from the saddle, towering above her. His handsome face was set in grim, bleak lines.

She waited. Finally he lifted his leg free of the stirrup, swung it around behind him, and leapt from the saddle. He closed the distance between them with long strides and stared down at her.

She faced him bravely, refusing to show fear, to let him have the satisfaction of knowing how desperately afraid for Lydie she felt.

Finally he spoke. "What are you doing here?"

"What have you done with Lydie? Where is she?"

"She is right . . . What do you mean what have I done with her?"

"No games, Crewe," she said wearily. "Where is she?"

"She is safe."

"Then let me see her."

"You shall, in good time."

"Curse you, Crewe! Where is she? Let me go to her at once. What have you done with her? Let me see my sister!"

Suddenly she advanced on him although she had never meant to and found that she was beating him with her fists. She butted her head against the unfair advantage of his strength and size. Tears streamed down her face, and her bonnet fell onto the ground, releasing her hair in a rippling cascade down her shoulders. "Where is she?" she screamed over and over again. "Where is she?"

"Easy, girl," Crewe said, trying to capture her arms and quiet her.

But fury made her quicksilver in his grasp, and she eluded him. Finally, in near desperation, he caught a handful of hair, and as she thrashed at him, she felt the jerk of his hold on her head and stopped, reaching behind her to pry his hands away.

He looked at her, her hands lifted behind her, her face tilted to him, standing within the curve of his arms, and cursed the foul business that set them at odds with each other.

He released her suddenly, and she toppled backward, stumbling to regain her footing, panting, her ineffectiveness revealed in the slump of her shoulders.

"Please, tell me where she is. I have the things from Grandmother's house. I have the snuffboxes. Please give me my sister."

"You did take them, then," Crewe said with something like sadness in his voice.

"Of course I did, what did you expect me to do, let you take Lydie away without lifting a finger to save her?"

"What has your stealing from your grandmother to do with Lydia?"

"I cannot imagine. What would you want with them when you are yourself so wealthy? I suppose it was just to confirm me a thief before my family. Is that what you wanted? But I would have done it and more to get Lydie back unharmed. Oh, tell me she is unharmed!" Once again Anna was helpless against the tears that flooded her eyes.

"Why did you send Lydie on a wild-goose chase to Farleigh Castle with George Ives?"

"Stop it! Where is she? I cannot stand this! Let me know at once where she is. Please. Please, Horace. Not for me, for her, please. She must be deeply frightened. She is just a child, you know. She has never been away from me. Please, where is she?"

"Very affecting. I am almost moved to believe you. But the truth is you sent her away for reasons I cannot begin to understand unless they were to cover your theft from your grandmother."

"You are talking nonsense. Where is she? Please."

"She is right behind you. Down at the end of the field, as far as the carriage could come."

Chapter
Nineteen

"SHE . . ."

Anna turned in the direction he had pointed and began running, reaching the woods, tripping and snagged by the heavy growth, sobbing, and crying over and over again, "Oh, Lydie." As the trees thinned, she saw a strange carriage, lost like a ship on the ocean, standing in the broad field, its path blocked by low undergrowth. The door was open, and George Ives stood talking to someone within. Seeing Anna dashing toward him, he said something, and immediately Lydia's head appeared. Then she was stumbling down the carriage steps, rushing to meet Anna. They embraced when they met and held each other fast.

Lydia's high spirits and laughter dimmed. "Annie, Annie, what is it? Oh, what is the matter, what has happened? Shhh. I'm here, shhh. Don't be so upset, Annie, dear. It was just a mixup. Shhh."

Anna's sobs quieted as she grew aware of something that was not quite right. Her sister was not upset; indeed,

Anna was the one who was distraught, and Lydia was in the unfamiliar role of comforter. Furthermore, she looked quite possessed and untroubled. Anna backed away, holding Lydia's arms. "You are all right? They haven't hurt you?"

"Of course I am all right. *Who* hasn't hurt me . . . George? George has not hurt me, Annie, in fact . . . we are betrothed!"

"Betrothed?"

"Yes, isn't it wonderful? It happened when we were at Farleigh Castle. Oh, Annie, the ruins were so romantic!"

"But you are too young to be engaged," said Anna, feeling unreal.

"Oh, I know. We will not announce it; it is just that we have decided it."

"I cannot allow it."

"Well, yes, Annie," soothed Lydia. "It is all right. We had all morning to talk, you see, and well, we really did try to talk of other things. It was bad enough not being chaperoned, but to be talking of getting married—but we did, and we decided . . ."

"You mean you have been with George Ives all day and there was no chaperon present?"

"Well, goodness, Annie! First you were sure I had been hurt or something, and now you are upset because I have not been chaperoned. And look at you! What has happened to you—you are covered with mud and sticks, your hair has come down, and you . . . Oh, Annie, what is it? Have you been hurt, is that why you didn't come to Farleigh Castle?"

"Oh, the devil take Farleigh Castle! What is going on? Why did you leave this morning? You were not abducted? But . . ." Anna spoke haltingly, feeling mixed parts victim, fool, villain, and sleepwalker.

"Abducted! Whatever are you talking about, Annie?"

"Your disappearance! You left the house before even the maids were up, you did not tell me or anyone else where you were going, then I got the note that unless I brought the snuffboxes ... It is not true," Anna realized, watching her sister's growing puzzlement and perplexity. "You were not abducted."

"No. I went to the castle because of your note telling me to go."

"*My* note?"

"Yes." Lydia returned to the coach and retrieved her reticule and drew from it a crumpled note that had obviously been folded and unfolded many times. Anna read it:

" 'Lydie, a surprise today—we are going to escape nurses and governess and have a treat. Now, you must get out of the house without arousing suspicion and get in the coach that will come for you by six o'clock. George will join you at the Green Goose Inn, and you will go to Farleigh Castle together where I will join you later. We will have a picnic and come back together. Now, keep this a secret, dear, or it will not happen. Anna.' "

"But I did not write this."

"It is in your hand, Annie. I know your hand."

Anna studied it. "Yes, it resembles my writing, but I did not write it. Why would I want to meet you at the castle? Why wouldn't we simply leave together? Besides, I am not sure you are even well enough to go to the castle."

"Of course I am, you goose. I have been, I have returned, and I am feeling quite well. But, Annie, you had to write it. It sounds exactly like you and it is in your hand. Why are you pretending you did not? Why didn't you come?"

"Lydie. I did not write it. I did not send you there. I got a note telling me you were abducted."

"Let me see it."

"I do not have it. It said I had to destroy it, so I burned it before I left the house."

"Ah!"

"Oh, Lydie, don't you distrust me, please."

Lydia hugged her. "Of course I do not distrust you. My lord, can you explain any of this?"

Anna had forgotten Horace Crewe, and she turned now to discover him standing with George, listening to the sisters. "I think it is probably someone's idea of a joke, Lydie."

"Joke!" exclaimed Anna. "Lydie, it was Horace who wrote the note. I can see he did not abduct you . . . but oh, this is all so confusing. He is here!" She turned on him challengingly. "How did you know I was here if you did not write that note and tell me to meet you here?"

"Easy. We asked at the stable, we asked peddlers and sweeps, linkboys, and a farmwife—we followed you."

"We?"

"All of us, Annie," said Lydia with a sweep of her hand to include herself and the two men. "We stopped at Grandmother's, and they said you were gone, but that you had dressed in your habit. Oh, and Grandmother said Grandfather's collection of snuffboxes had been stolen— isn't that terrible! But as I was saying, I wanted to find you, and go to the Wilcoxes', but everyone wanted me to rest, but I would not and so we all went, except Burleigh, who said he would not lift a finger for you—he is very angry, Annie, but I could not figure out what about . . . and so here we are. Now we must return and get you cleaned up."

Anna stared at her younger sister, at her authority and composure, trying to puzzle out the truth. She looked helplessly at George and Horace, trying to read in their faces some hint as to the truth behind the day's confusion and lies.

Horace stepped forward. "I do think you should return, Lydie. You must be tired. George can take you back. Now, do not worry," he said to her as she started to protest, "I will bring your sister along as soon as we locate her horse . . ."

"I'll go with Lydie . . ."

"What about the snuffboxes? Let her go on ahead," he said.

Anna stared at him, trapped. "Very well. You return," she said, and nodded at Lydia and George. "I will be perfectly fine and will follow shortly."

Lydia and Anna hugged, and then the carriage made its way teetering and heaving over the rough terrain back to the road. Anna turned to Horace.

"You got rid of her," she said.

"Yes."

"What is it you do not wish her to hear?"

"Not hear, see."

"What?"

Horace strode over to her, clamped his hand firmly behind her back and pressed her to him, seeking her lips with his, forcing her head back, and kissed her deeply, hard, and long.

"Horace!"

"I have been wanting to do that for the longest time."

Anna laughed. "I cannot believe this is me. That I am here with you. You are either a charlatan or a horrible prankster. You have got me into a terrible situation with my grandmother, having stolen her things with no more of a reason now than a confusing tissue of lies could produce, and yet I find enough favor with you that you plant kisses on me!"

Laughing, she ran back through the woods. He came after her, not hurrying to catch up with her or to restrain her. She pulled the bundle from under the bush, and standing on her tiptoes, slipped the loop over the pommel. Stroking the horse's long face, she led it into the clearing where Horace stood.

She realized he was making no effort to untie his own horse or to mount it. She allowed her hand to slip from the horse's reins.

She watched Horace, and he looked at her. They were alone on the grassy verge.

She went up to him. "Horace," she said huskily.

"Annie."

She pressed herself to him and lifted her mouth to his. Immediately he consumed her in an intense embrace that pressed every fiber of her being to him, that caused her body to tighten and yearn for his.

"Horace," she murmured again as she kissed his face, his neck, as she reached with her hands to his head and buried her fingers in his thick black hair. She looked at him with love and desire.

He caressed her head with his hand, drawing his hand slowly down her silken cheek, her flowing hair, down her arm, her waist, to her hip. "Annie, will you marry me?"

"Yes."

He kissed her again. "Now, let us leave, little one."

"No."

"There will be time for this later, Annie."

"But I cannot wait. I never can wait. I do not like waiting for things."

Horace drew back his head and laughed. "That is an understatement, my impetuous one. Ah, Annie, I love you."

He lifted her in his arms, strode into the woods, and laid her on a gentle slope—and against the rush of water they made love.

Anna lay on the grass and looked into the trees, at the patterns of branches and leaves against the sky. She felt wanton and loose-limbed. She turned to watch Horace, who was untying the horses. "Come, my lazy one, time to face the music."

Smiling, she rose and shook leaves from her clothes and hair. She twisted her hair up onto her head and reached for the bonnet he held out, and, holding her hair with one hand, slipped it onto her head so that it held her hair in place. Then she raised herself onto her tiptoes and kissed him again. She turned to mount her horse, but he took her shoulders and gently drew her around and kissed her. They stood locked, leaning into the snickering, shifting horses, and then finally, with loving looks, separated, remounted, and began the long ride into Bath.

They did not converse. They did not try to sort out the events that had shaped this topsy-turvy day. Anna was lost in a dream of well-being and happiness. Nothing seemed real to her. Not his love for her, not the weight of the bundle against her leg, not Lydie's adventures of the morning, not her grandmother's confusion, and not her cousin's outrage.

All that would come soon enough. Now she could only ride as carefully as possible, avoiding holes in the road, not running into low stone walls, while all the while watching Horace, smiling at him, studying every detail of his face.

He laughed and told her they would both end in a ditch if she did not attend to her horse. Then he laughed again and said that was how he had first kissed her, wasn't it? Someday they were going to have to try a kiss that was completely unconnected with ditches and damp ground.

She laughed, and they looked at each other joyously, not believing their love. But Horace did not have to close out the future as Anna did. For him their lovemaking had not been the seizing of the last sweet thing before a threatening future.

Chapter Twenty

WHEN THEY ARRIVED at the Crescent, they were directed by a stern and tight-lipped Craig into the green parlor, where the countess, Burleigh, Lydia, George, and Miss Bennet all awaited them. Lady Tretham greeted them curtly and nodded a dismissal to George and Crewe, but Horace spoke.

"If you can indulge me just this once, Lady Tretham, and allow me to stay."

"But, Horace, we have family matters to discuss here which I should not wish you to hear."

"I have probably heard them already, madam," he said, regarding her steadily.

She flushed. "Be that as it may, Horace, I cannot allow you to become embroiled in them."

"I am afraid I am already deeply embroiled. You see, I have just asked for your granddaughter's hand in marriage and have been accepted. So I am about to be embroiled in your family's affairs, no matter what."

There was an outburst following his announcement. Lydia exclaimed in pleasure. Burleigh's jaw flew open, and he muttered an expletive. Anna blushed and glanced up at Horace, who was smiling.

The countess shook her head and replied. "Earlier I would have been delighted, but now, Horace, I cannot be. Things are not right, and I do not wish to discuss them with you."

"You mean about your granddaughter being a thief."

"So you know." She turned to Anna, puzzled. "Did you tell him?"

"Horace has always known the worst of me, Grandmother," Anna replied, coming as close to the truth about the stickpin as she ever would with her grandmother.

"Then you did take the jewels and the snuffboxes."

"No, only the latter. And here they are," she said, picking up the bundle she had dropped on a chair and giving it to her grandmother.

Then she turned and let herself collapse into a chair. Lydia was watching her with a look of radiant joy and glanced at Horace to include him in it. Anna summoned up a responsive smile.

"You think you can settle it just like that?" said Burleigh, speaking for the first time. "Returning what you stole does not alter the fact that you stole them."

"No, of course it does not, Burleigh. I did not steal them. I took them in order to secure Lydie's release."

"Release!" said Burleigh scornfully.

"I know. I was tricked. Someone wrote me a note saying Lydie had been abducted, and if I brought the snuffboxes, she would be freed. I went to the place where I was to meet her abductors, but no one came until Lydie herself came, with Horace and George—and she was quite safe, obviously not having been abducted. So there was no reason for me to steal them. It was all a trick or a joke."

"Hardly a joke, Anna," Burleigh said. "You might be able to account for the snuffboxes in this way, but not for the ruby or the diadem. What do you have to say about them?"

"Nothing, Burleigh, but for repeating that I did not take them."

"Then who did?"

"I do not know."

"Well, madam," Burleigh said, turning to his grandmother, "I hope you do not believe this faradiddle. Pretending she took these things to ransom Lydia. It is obvious that they were both in on it. No doubt she wrote that note to Lydia so that Lydia would be out of the way, and then Lydia's absence gave her a reason to have committed the theft if she were caught. As she was when Crewe followed her."

Anna was dismayed by the plausibility of his story. So, apparently, was her grandmother, who regarded her with very sad eyes.

"I'll wager you planned this between you, didn't you, before you even came," Burleigh continued. "Even using a 'governess' as a respectable cover—how you would move to Bath, rob your grandmother with both extravagant purchases and thefts, and then disappear. But you did not succeed.

"Pretending that Lydia was ill—she has not been ill a day in her life, has she? Your game was uncovered when Mr. Gibson said she had no disease."

"No . . ."

"You are just like your mother," Burleigh went on, "aren't you, Anna? She was a spendthrift who drove her husband to gambling and drink, to sell secrets to the French."

"Enough, Burleigh!" the countess said. "I think there is a limit to how much even I will allow Louisa to be made the villain. She had been dead for five years before my son's death. Whatever drinking and gambling he did—yes, and even selling military secrets—he did himself. My son."

Burleigh was visibly disconcerted. He resumed the original focus of his attack. "Then what do you say about Lydia and her so-called illness?"

Lydia sat white-faced on the edge of a small chaise. She suddenly got to her feet. Anna went to her side protectively, but Lydia held up her hand and bade her stand back.

"My illness has been a burden to everyone. To my sister," she said, looking at Anna, "and to Benny." She nodded at her in acknowledgment. "For years I was weak, unable to grow, unable to take part in the daily activities of life. Then I came here. Mr. Gibson has told me that he thinks I recovered because I am no longer a burden to anyone and because at last I have a home. My illness, he has persuaded me, was caused by sorrow and was a form of mourning for my mother."

Anna blinked back tears, and the countess took Lydia in her arms and held her tightly. "Oh, my girls," she said, drawing Anna into the embrace.

"Very affecting," Burleigh said with a sneer, "but balderdash if I have ever heard of it. Whoever heard of someone becoming sick because she was sad! The truth is, you feigned it to work your way into my grandmother's affections, gain her trust, and then rob her."

"Oh, that is not true, Burleigh. We came for Lydie."

"But you spent money like there was no end to it. Can you deny that?"

"Yes, I spent money—on clothes and books and pets and . . . And I would spend it all again. I enjoyed it!" Anna looked defiantly around the room.

"That is all too obvious," Burleigh said.

"Hold on, Burleigh," said Lady Tretham, resuming her seat. "No one begrudges Anna her shopping sprees. I would have insisted she be well turned out, no matter what the cost. Anyway, what Anna has spent has been negligible, and it was a pleasure to watch her assume such a distinctive style. She has a great deal more than you, you know. Is that why you are so jealous of her?

"But her spending is not the point," she continued, "the point is the thefts. If Anna did steal these things, then that is criminal and another matter."

"But I did not, and Lydie did not—Miss Bennet—none of us did."

"Then who did?" Burleigh shot back.

"I do not know. I truly do not know." Anna sat back down, feeling her knees weaken.

"Enough." Horace stepped forward and laid a hand on Anna's shoulder. "I will not allow you to badger her further, Burleigh. She is innocent, and you know she is. As only you, in fact, can know she is."

"And what is that supposed to mean, Crewe?"

"You know."

"No, I do not know. I do not know what your game is with Anna. It is probably some scheme you have worked out between you. Given her father's morals, I do not suppose hers are any better—what has she done, paid you for your silence with her favors?"

Horace tensed and would have struck Burleigh, except for Anna's intense, blushing mortification at his side.

"I will not bother to challenge you on that, Burleigh. Lady Anna will soon be my wife and protected from your cruelties to her. They are at an end."

"What cruelties?"

"Oh, Horace, you do not know what you are saying," Anna interrupted him. "Burleigh has not inflicted any cruelties on me. On the contrary, he has helped me, he has shielded me from the creditors, protected Papa's name—he even offered for me!"

"Offered for you?" Horace repeated blankly. "When was that?"

"Well, the morning the roses came. When we were together and you gave me that . . . that . . . pretty stickpin . . ."

"That you had stolen from him!" Burleigh shouted, triumphant. "I heard you! I heard you tell him you had stolen it and did not deserve it! You see," he said, wheeling around to the countess, "she had stolen already even before she came to Bath—and she stole when she got here. She is a thief through and through."

Lady Tretham asked, "What is this about, Anna?"

Anna opened her mouth to speak, but Horace cut in. "Allow me to answer, Lady Tretham. Anna and I had a joke between us, a dare. She has stolen nothing—but my heart," he said, smiling down at her.

Burleigh expostulated. "That is not true, that is not what I heard. She said she stole it, and you said she could have it, that it was the first of all the things you would give her . . ." He broke off abruptly.

"Yes, Burleigh?" Horace asked coolly.

"Nothing."

"Nothing? You guessed I was going to offer for Anna, didn't you? Is that why you interrupted us—and then immediately offered for her yourself?"

"No!"

"But, yes," Anna said, rising. "Yes, that is what happened. He asked me immediately . . ."

"And you refused him?"

"Yes, of course."

"And that day the ruby was found to be missing?"

"Yes," Anna answered in a trance of memory.

"And then the diadem was found in your chamber?"

"Yes."

Horace turned to Burleigh. "You wanted Anna for yourself, and when you could not have her, you tried to destroy her, didn't you?"

Burleigh sputtered. "No."

"Yes," Horace said. "And why? Because you are in desperate need of money, and Anna's claim on her grandmother had to be destroyed, either through marriage so that you could control her inheritance, or by having her grandmother repudiate her."

"Nonsense!" Burleigh strutted to the mantel. "Look at me!" he cried, pointing to his clothes and jewels. "Do I look like a poor man?"

"No, but I would wager that every farthing you have is on your back."

Burleigh stuck out his chin pugnaciously.

Horace lazily raised his hand. "No, Burleigh, your threats will have no effect on me. I am well aware of your brawls."

Burleigh drew himself up. "Well, Crewe," he said with a sneer, "if you cannot back up your insults, you can leave."

"I shall leave in good time. Let us go over the facts. One, Dragonsmere was impoverished when you took it over. George?"

George, who had been sitting next to Lydia on the chaise, turned to Anna and spoke modestly.

"I talked to Gates, your former bailiff . . ."

Anna nodded.

"Burleigh pensioned him off, but we found him through his daughter, who lives near Dragonsmere. There were no debts, according to him. The earl had gambled, but never in such a way as to endanger the estates. They were profitable when he died."

"But the creditors . . ."

"There were no creditors, Lady Anna. That was simply an invention of Burleigh's to get you out of the way."

"But that is not true," she said, "They have come to my grandmother, who has been generous enough to pay them."

"Stuff and nonsense, girl. There have been no creditors to dun me."

Anna looked from her grandmother to Burleigh. "But you said . . ."

"Yes, Anna."

"There were no creditors at all? No reason we had to hide in Yorkshire so they could not track us down?"

"No," Horace said quietly.

"That's not true," sputtered Burleigh, "I paid off most of them."

"Cut line, Burleigh. Gates has shown us his copies of the ledgers. But it is true Dragonsmere has gone to rack and ruin—but only since you took it over. Isn't that right?"

"No! Well, I could use some money," he said, throwing a look toward his grandmother.

Horace continued. "And you have been here in Bath living off your grandmother, haven't you? You are the real sponger, aren't you, Burleigh?"

"But, Horace," Anna asked, turning to him, "Burleigh knows my grandmother has no real money. There is no point in Burleigh pursuing me for her money—or any of this. He has been protecting her. He knows her generosity to me is probably unwise. She has nothing but some small investments and will run through them soon."

The countess snorted with laughter. "That is quite true. Small investments. Come, girl, do not be a ninny. My investments total several hundred thousand pounds. Enough to cover a few gowns, I think."

"But Burleigh said . . ."

"Burleigh knows nothing of my affairs."

"He says he advises you."

Lady Tretham snorted again. "McClain at the bank advises me, as he advised my husband."

Anna gazed sadly at Burleigh. "I was fifteen when my father died. I knew nothing about the world, and I believed everything you said. I trusted you. But now I see I have listened to you too many times. All you have ever done is lie to me."

"Nonsense. It is you who lies. You are a liar and a thief."

"Yes, what of the thefts?" the countess asked.

"What of them, Burleigh?" Horace asked.

"What do you mean? Ask her!"

"No, I shall tell you. Or George."

George said, "The ruby was pawned in Bristol. I brought it back yesterday. It is at Crewe's rooms at the Paragon. The pawnbroker is willing to testify to the appearance of the rather portly gentleman who brought it in."

"No!" Anna whispered.

"Yes. When all is said and done, Lady Tretham," Horace said, "the thefts amount only to the ruby, which has been recovered. The diadem and the snuffboxes were never taken. They were used only to entrap Anna, about whom Burleigh then carefully spread rumors throughout Bath so that she would be disgraced and you would be forced to repudiate her."

"But the business with Lydie, leaving the notes . . ." Anna asked.

"You arranged all that, didn't you, Burleigh, so that Anna would be caught red-handed and no one would believe her?"

"But I saw the note—it was in my handwriting. And whoever sent it knew where I went riding. Ah, but you knew that, and you could have copied my hand . . ." Anna looked sadly at Burleigh.

There was a silence. Burleigh broke in. "You would believe the daughter of a traitor?"

"Stop!" Lydia put her hands to her ears. "Do not speak a word against my father . . ."

"But it is true, Lydie. No matter what else . . ." Anna said quietly.

"No, Anna, it is not true. These thefts, the lies, the squandering of the estate, even your retreat in Yorkshire, none of those comes near to what your cousin did to your father."

Crewe stood straight, looking at Burleigh, now pale, leaning against a chair.

"You murdered Edward Farrant, Earl of Tretham."

There was an explosion of cries and exclamations in the room.

"Murdered him! Now your wits are addled, Crewe. Edward killed himself."

"Yes, he pulled the trigger, but you engineered it. This will be the hardest part of all," he said, turning to the countess, Anna, and Lydia.

"Lord Tretham is supposed to have sold the plans of the Sea Fencibles to Bevaqua, who pretended to be in the payment of the French. George and I discovered an associate of Burleigh's who was there that evening and was willing to talk. Burleigh had made the mistake of going to Dragonsmere and summoning him down to Bath for help in discrediting Anna. I saw him at the concert in the Assembly Rooms."

Anna remembered the feral-looking man.

"One of your mistakes, for it made me even more suspicious. Odd, Burleigh, how your own behavior led to your downfall. Going to such lengths to humiliate Anna publicly about her clothes, her card-playing, telling me of her father's perfidy. Why would you speak against your benefactor or your cousin? That made me initially suspicious, and then bringing that man to a public place. George and I had a long chat with him in my rooms where he is, alas, quite unable to move about freely. Have you been wondering where he is, Burleigh?"

Burleigh was purple in the face.

"Lefferts has told us some things that shed light on Tretham's last days. First that party, at which he supposedly told the plans, took place in a private gambling den which had been cleared of all other customers but yourself, Lefferts, a man named Wiggens, also in your pay, and Bevaqua, the so-called spy, and Anna's father."

"That is not true, there were many other gentlemen there as well. I could give you their names."

"You may have bribed others to say they were there. No doubt I could discover that quite easily. But the fact is you doctored the earl's wine with laudanum, and he passed out and was unconscious most of the evening."

"That is not true," Burleigh blustered.

"When he came to, you told him he had divulged the plans to Bevaqua and been paid for them. He, not being able to remember, and trusting you, believed you."

"No, that cannot be—Burleigh could not do such a thing!" cried Anna.

"But he did."

George added, "I am afraid it is true, Lady Anna. Lefferts told us that when Lord Tretham regained consciousness, Burleigh told him what had happened, one of his cronies backed him up, and there was nothing left for your father but to believe it."

"That's a damned lie!"

"So your father," Horace continued grimly, "told he had confided state secrets, coming to and discovering a fat roll of bills on him that Burleigh had placed there, was convinced he was a traitor. And he killed himself."

"None of this is true!" Burleigh shrieked.

"But why?" Anna asked, ignoring her cousin's outburst.

"To inherit Dragonsmere."

"But he would have inherited it anyway!"

"He was too deeply in debt to wait."

"Burleigh," said the Countess of Tretham, rising to her feet, pointing her finger at her grandson and speaking in a shaking, hoarse voice, "get out of my house. Now. Never come back. Leave England immediately. If I ever find out that you have returned, I will see you hanged."

The silence in the room was dreadful. Burleigh, white as paper, looked from one face to another and found nothing that promised mercy. Finally he bolted to the door.

They watched him leave in silence.

Finally Lydia spoke. "Father was not a spy."

"No," said Anna, going to her and taking her hand.

They stood together. "But we lost him."

"Yes," Anna replied. "Burleigh robbed us of our father. But, Lydie, he was not happy. His life was a burden to him."

Lydia squeezed her hand, showing she understood.

Lady Tretham, who seemed shrunken and desolate, spoke with a voice that still held authority. "This is enough. We must rest. I must rest, anyway. And you, my dear," she said, indicating Lydia.

"But first I want to say my son is dead. Because I was a fool, he was dead to me longer than he need have been. But I have his daughters, who are treasures to me. And now, just as I have got them, it seems they are both in a hurry to marry and leave me," she added with a ghost of a twinkle in her eye.

The young women hugged her in turn. "Not for a few years, Grandmother," Lydia said. "I shall be here with you until then."

"Well, my dear," she said, turning to Anna and placing her hand on her cheek, "your welcome in Bath has been harsh and a severe trial to you. But you have found happiness. You could not have chosen a better man in England, even if he is the son of my best friend."

Anna smiled. Then, putting her arm around Lydia, the countess left the room. Miss Bennet followed, after exchanging a quick hug with Anna. George shook hands with Horace and congratulated Anna, then left quietly.

Anna and Horace were alone.

Anna sat bleak and silent. Horace watched her, giving her time to absorb all she had learned.

Finally she raised her head to him. "We have each other," she said with a tremulous smile.

He lifted her to him, and they clung to each other.

"Oh, Horace, will I ever be able to adjust to everything that has happened today?"

"Well, I hope you will come to be very familiar with one of the things that happened today," he said, smiling.

She blushed furiously and buried her face in his shirt-front.

He laughed outright. "Ah, my shy, modest Anna." He lifted her chin. "I am a very happy man."

"Yes," she said, smiling radiantly.

"What a very odd courtship we have had," he reflected.

She laughed. "It was certainly not love at first sight."

"Oh, but it was! Do you not remember that I kissed you before you had even regained consciousness or uttered a single word?"

"Oh, no, you cannot get away with that! Come now, remember how you described me to Mrs. Ives?"

"Ah . . . no . . ."

"Oh, yes, you do." Anna laughed. "I was a 'vulgar shrew with more hair than wit.' "

Horace grinned. "I was wrong."

Anna snuggled against him contentedly. "What do you love best about me?"

"Well, not your driving."

"No."

"Not your conversation in the ballroom."

"No?"

"I guess it would have to be . . . yes . . . the way you waltz!"

Anna's laugh was interrupted by a kiss, a long passionate kiss full of future promise.